CW00840158

The Invisible Boy

Sally Gardner is the author and illustrator of
The Fairy Catalogue, A Book of Princesses and other
popular books for children. She started out
as a designer of sets and costumes for the theatre.
She has a son and twin daughters and lives in London.

To Dominic
with very happy memories of Splodge

The Invisible Boy

Sally Gardner

Orion
Children's Books

This omnibus edition first published in Great Britain in 2007
by Orion Children's Books
a division of the Orion Publishing Group Ltd
Orion House
5 Upper St Martin's Lane
London WC2H 9EA
First published by Orion Children's Books as two separate volumes:
The Invisible Boy first published in Great Britain 2002
The Boy with the Magic Numbers first published in Great Britain 2003

1 3 5 7 9 10 8 6 4 2

Text and illustrations copyright © Sally Gardner 2002, 2003

The moral rights of the author have been asserted.

All rights reserved. No part of this publication may be reproduced, stored
in a retrieval system, or transmitted, in any form or by any means,
electronic, mechanical, photocopying, recording or otherwise, without the
prior permission of Orion Children's Books.

The Orion Publishing Group's policy is to use papers that are natural,
renewable and recyclable products and made from wood grown in
sustainable forests. The logging and manufacturing processes are expected
to conform to the environmental regulations of the country of origin.

A catalogue record for this book is available from the British Library
Printed in Great Britain by Clays Ltd, St Ives plc

ISBN   978 1 84255 613 9

www.orionbooks.co.uk

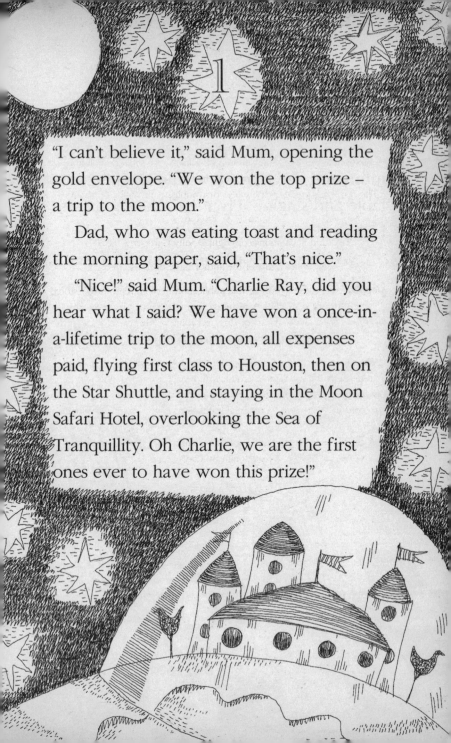

"I can't believe it," said Mum, opening the gold envelope. "We won the top prize – a trip to the moon."

Dad, who was eating toast and reading the morning paper, said, "That's nice."

"Nice!" said Mum. "Charlie Ray, did you hear what I said? We have won a once-in-a-lifetime trip to the moon, all expenses paid, flying first class to Houston, then on the Star Shuttle, and staying in the Moon Safari Hotel, overlooking the Sea of Tranquillity. Oh Charlie, we are the first ones ever to have won this prize!"

Dad dropped his toast and paper.

"Let me see," he said. "Oh Lily my love, I don't believe it. We are going to the moon!"

Sam walked into the room to find his mum and dad dancing round the kitchen table and singing "Fly me to the moon and let me play among the stars."

"What's going on?" said Sam, who was only half awake and unused to seeing his parents singing quite so loudly on a Saturday morning.

They told him the good news, both excited and talking at once, so that it took quite some time before they realised that children under twelve weren't allowed. It meant quite simply that Sam couldn't go.

"Well, that's that," said Dad after Mum had phoned to double-check with Dream Maker Tours.

"I will be fine," said Sam bravely. "Look, you must go. It's only for two weeks and I have lots of friends I can go and stay with, like Billy. I'm sure his mum won't mind."

2

The great day arrived. Mum and Dad were packed and ready to go when the phone rang. It was Billy Brand's mother, who was terribly sorry to say that Billy was not at all well. The doctor had just come round and said he had a very infectious virus. Sam couldn't possibly stay with him now. Mrs Brand hoped it hadn't ruined their trip.

"What are we going to do?" said Mum, putting down the last of the suitcases.

"I don't know," said Dad.

Just then the doorbell rang. Dad answered it. He was surprised to find their next-door neighbour, Mrs Hilda Hardbottom, standing there.

"I just popped round to see if you wanted the plants watering while you were away," she said, smiling.

"That's very kind of you,

Mrs Hardbottom, but I don't think we will
be going after all," said Dad.

"What?" said Hilda, walking uninvited
into the hall and closing the front door
behind her. "Not going on a once-in-a-
lifetime trip to the moon! Why not?"

Mum felt a bit silly. She should have got
this better organised. "Sam's friend's mum
has just rang to say he's not at all well, so
Sam can't go to stay there," she said.

"Oh dear," said Mrs Hardbottom. "Still,
that shouldn't stop you. Anyway you can't
cancel, not now, with the eyes of the
world on you, so to speak."

"We really have no choice, I can't leave Sam alone," said Mum.

"We must phone Dream Maker Tours right away and tell them we can't go," said Dad.

"There is no need to cancel. If it comes to that I can look after Sam," said Mrs Hardbottom firmly.

Mum and Dad were lost for words. They felt somewhat embarrassed. Mr and Mrs Hardbottom were their neighbours, and had been for years, but they really knew nothing about them, except they kept to themselves and seemed nice enough.

It was Sam who broke the awkward silence.

"That's the answer, Dad," he said, trying to sound cheerful.

Mum and Dad looked at one another then at Sam. Oh, how they loved their little boy! It broke their hearts seeing him being so grown-up and courageous.

"It's very kind of you, Mrs Hardbottom, but…"

"Hilda," said Mrs Hardbottom, taking control of the situation. At that moment the doorbell rang. "No more buts," said Hilda, opening the front door as if it were her own house.

Plunket Road looked barely recognisable.
It was full of wellwishers and TV cameras.
Parked outside their front door was a
white shining limousine waiting to take
the Rays away.

A TV presenter with a games show
face walked into the hall where Mum and
Dad were standing. They both looked like
a couple of startled rabbits caught in the
headlights of an oncoming circus lorry.

"Mr and Mrs Ray, today is your day!
You are Dream Maker's out-of-this-world
winners!" said the presenter. "How does it
feel?"

Dad and Mum appeared to be frozen to the spot.

"Yes," said the presenter, "I too would be lost for words if I was lucky enough to be going to the moon."

Hilda spoke up. "They are a little sad to be leaving their son. But he is going to be fine, me and Ernie are going to look after him."

The camera panned on to Sam's face.

"You must be his kind and devoted granny," said the presenter, pleased at least that someone in the family had a voice.

"No," said Hilda, "I am the next door neighbour."

The presenter beamed his most plastic smile and his teeth shone like a neon sign. "Now isn't that what neighbours are for!" he said, putting an arm round Hilda and Sam.

Hilda was in heaven at being seen by forty million viewers world-wide. Mum and Dad smiled weakly. Nothing was agreed. This was all moving too fast.

"I brought round a disposable camera," Hilda continued. "I was hoping that my dear friends Charlie and Lily would take some nice pictures of the Sea of Tranquillity, for my Ernie. He wants to know what watersports they have up there on the moon."

"Well, isn't this cosy," said the presenter, handing the camera to Mum. He was now moving Mum and Dad out of the house into a sea of flashing camera lights, and somewhere in amongst all the chaos that was whirling around them, they found themselves parted from Sam. The white limousine whisked them away. The last thing they could see was Sam waving bravely.

4

There were two things at the top of Hilda Hardbottom's wish list. They had been there for forty years and hadn't until today shown any sign of coming true. The first was to be on TV, the second was to be rich.

"I don't know what's come over you, sweetpea, you hate boys," said Ernie in a stage whisper after Sam had gone to bed. "You always said they smelt of old socks that had been chewed by a dog."

"There is no need to whisper, Ernie Hardbottom, unless I say whisper," she snapped back at him.

Sam, who was trying to get to sleep upstairs in the cold spare bedroom with no curtains, heard Hilda's voice, and crept to the top of the landing to see what was going on. What he heard made going to sleep even harder.

"Because, you numskull, how else was I ever going to star on TV?" said Hilda. "You have videotaped it, haven't you?"

"Yes, every minute of it, dearest," said Ernie.

"Good," said Hilda. Then she added as an afterthought, "Sam's parents must have taken out a lot of travel insurance, don't you think?"

"Well, if they haven't, Dream Maker Tours would have done, I imagine," said Ernie, pressing the play button on the video machine.

"Just think if anything were to go wrong with that Star Shuttle! Think of all that insurance money," said Hilda, rubbing her hands together with glee.

"That's not very nice," said Ernie.

"Who said anything about being nice," said Hilda, a wicked grin spreading across her face.

17

Sam went back to his cold lumpy bed.
Tears welled up in his eyes. Oh, how he
hoped that nothing would go wrong and
that his mum and dad would soon be
safely home!

The next day Sam went back to school
and only had to be with Hilda and Ernie
in the evening. All the evenings were long
and dull. There was never enough to eat.
After tea they would all sit together
watching TV, and Hilda would hand out
some of her homemade treacle toffee. The
first night Sam had been so hungry that
he had made the mistake of taking a piece.
To his horror his mouth seemed to stick

together so he could hardly swallow, let alone speak. All he could do was sit there trying to finish the treacle toffee while listening to Ernie snoring and Hilda's stomach gurgling like an old dishwasher.

Bedtime couldn't come soon enough. Every night Sam would thank the stars that it was one day nearer to his mum and dad coming home.

But then, on the day his parents were due to return to earth, the unthinkable happened. Houston said they had lost all contact with the Star Shuttle. They were hoping it was just computer failure. The slow, mournful hours passed and the Star Shuttle still couldn't be found. Finally a spokesman for Dream Maker Tours announced on the six o'clock news that the Star Shuttle was missing.

5

The next morning Sam got ready to go to school. He would tell his teachers that he couldn't stay with the Hardbottoms any longer. He had lots of friends at school. He was sure someone would help him while this terrible mess was sorted out.

Hilda must have known what he was planning, for she was waiting for him by the front door, wearing her iron face. "Where do you think you're off to?"

"School," said Sam.

"No you're not. It's out of the question. Not at this sad time," said Hilda firmly.

"I can't stay here, I mean I was only supposed to be with you until my mum and dad got home," said Sam.

"Well, they're not home, are they, so it looks as if you're stuck with us," Hilda said smugly.

"But…" said Sam.

"The buts will have to make their own toast," said Hilda, pushing him back upstairs into his room.

The next few days passed in a haze. Hilda didn't allow him to go to school, or even out of the house alone, not with all the press and TV camped in their front garden. Sam Ray's parents were a hot story. Sam's picture appeared on every TV, newspaper, and Internet site in the world. Sam just remembered flashing lights and Hilda and Ernie being called the nation's favourite neighbours.

After a nailbiting week had passed, the officials at Houston said the Star Shuttle had been lost in space. All on board were presumed dead.

That was that. No more exciting pictures to be had. The TV and pressmen packed up and left.

Sam and his parents became yesterday's story. Old newspapers blowing around with the dead autumn leaves, and like them a thing of the past.

6

Hilda had liked the idea of being the nation's favourite neighbour and had made the most of it. She wore a kind and caring face that made the press and friends of the Rays say Sam was lucky to have Mr and Mrs Hardbottom to look after him. Especially as there were no living relatives.

But behind the thin disguise, Hilda was making plans. She had rented a cheap bungalow by the sea and made Ernie write a letter to Sam's school saying that they were taking Sam away on holiday, so that he would have a chance to get over his sad loss.

Hilda's plan was simple, and that was to get her hands on the Rays' insurance money. She wouldn't be able to do that if Sam said he didn't want to stay with them, and she couldn't keep him locked up forever. No, the best thing was to get right away. There were too many people offering to help. Mr Jenkins, who had mended Ernie's Ford Cortina, had said only the other week that he and his family would gladly look after Sam.

Ernie was a bit puzzled as to why Hilda was so keen to keep him.

"Why are you going to all the trouble and expense of booking a seaside holiday?" he asked. "We never go away."

"Because we can't stay here. People will begin to ask questions," said Hilda firmly.

"About what?" said Ernie scratching his head.

24

"About who is going to look after Sam," said Hilda beginning to lose her temper. "We don't want him saying he doesn't like it here."

"I'm sure he doesn't," said Ernie. "We can't look after him. We don't know anything about boys."

Hilda bristled like an old hairbrush. "I am only going to say this once more Ernie Hardbottom, and if it doesn't sink in to that sievelike brain of yours you can go and live in the potting shed with your CB radio for all I care."

Ernie looked at Hilda. She was not a pretty sight.

"The Rays," she said, talking to him as if he were five years old, "were insured for a lot of money by Dream Maker Tours, and now they are dead that money will go to Sam. Or to be more precise, to the guardians of Sam.

"If we play our cards right, that will be you and me."

"So we are going to adopt Sam," said Ernie, still not quite sure what Hilda was up to. "Don't you think, dearest, we are a little too old to be bringing up a boy?"

Hilda looked at Ernie as a cat might look at a mouse. "No," she said, "it means, you peabrain, that we are going to be rich."

"How do you make that out, sweetpea?" said Ernie, looking even more puzzled. "It's Sam's money, after all, and I don't think he would want to give it to us."

Hilda sighed. "I sometimes wonder how with a brain as small as yours you manage to keep going at all."

"That's not fair dearest," said Ernie in a small hurt voice.

"Oh, for pity's sake, life's not fair," said Hilda. "It is going to be our money and once we get our hands on it we are off to where the sun shines bright. Personally I am going to live the life I deserve. Sam can go whistle for his supper, and so can you if you don't buck up your ideas."

Ernie knew it was pointless to argue with Hilda. Once she got an idea in her head, it wasn't so much like watching a bull, rather a ten-ton lorry go through a china shop. Nothing was going to stop her.

7

That night Sam was unable to sleep. He looked out of his curtainless window at the back garden, with its neat rows of pumpkins, its potting shed, and its garden gnomes, lit up in the moonlight. He could even see the treehouse that Dad and he had made in his garden next door.

Sam flashed his torch up into the starry night sky. He had never felt more

abandoned. Space seemed to him so everlastingly vast. Where did it end? He felt tiny and invisible.

Sam lay down and tried to get to sleep. Suddenly there was a loud crash outside. He sat up in bed. All was quiet in the house. Sam was sure that if it had been an important crash, Hilda and Ernie would be up in a flash, but nothing stirred. Sam looked out of the window again. Everything looked the same, except that something was glowing in the pumpkin patch.

Sam tiptoed past Hilda and Ernie's bedroom. The door was ajar and Hilda's snores were loud enough to cover the noise of the creaking stairs. He went down to the back door and managed with great difficulty to get it open. He felt somewhat stupid standing in the garden, in the middle of the night, in his slippers and pyjamas. If he was caught now he would be in big trouble.

He walked slowly down the garden path. There, among the gnomes and the prize pumpkins, was what looked like a metal salad washer. A little like the one Hilda used to clean lettuce in, but bigger and a lot fancier. Whirring sounds were coming from it.

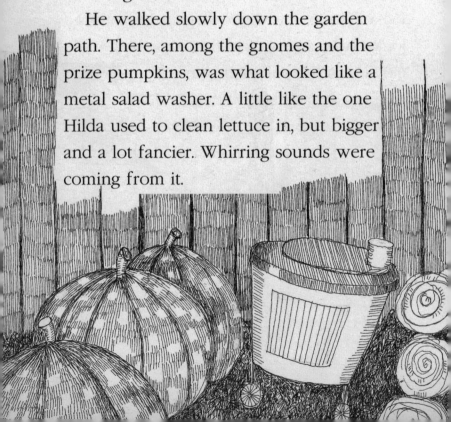

Then, to his horror, a gust of wind blew the back door shut. He turned the handle, but it wouldn't budge. He was locked out.

Things were not looking good. This is most definitely a dream, thought Sam. For there, walking about bowing to the garden gnomes, was an alien with green and splodgy skin, saying, "Hello, I come in peas. Take me to your chef."

When the gnomes didn't reply, the little alien, who was only a bit bigger than them, adjusted the two long pink tufts that stuck out of the top of his head and started again. "Hello, I come in peas…"

"Can I help?" asked Sam.

8

The little alien looked up, not in the least bit put off by someone so much bigger than himself. "My name is Splodge," he said. "I am from Planet Ten Rings. I come in peas."

"Good to see you. I am Sam Ray," said Sam.

"Are you the big chef?" asked Splodge.

"No," said Sam, "I am just a boy. I don't cook."

Splodge looked at him and then said, "One milacue, please." He ran back to where the metal salad washer lay and went inside.

"If this is a dream," said Sam to himself, "then why does it all seem so real?"

"Chief," said the alien, coming out, "take me to your chief."

"If you mean Mrs Hilda Hardbottom," said Sam, "I don't think she would be too pleased to see you."

Splodge leant on a flowerpot and muttered to himself. Then, pointing to the garden gnomes, he said, "Who are all those people? Are they prisoners of the Bottom?"

"No," said Sam, "they are plastic, I think, and they don't talk. They are just there to decorate the garden."

Splodge started to make a funny noise and for one awful moment Sam thought he was choking. He was not up on alien first aid. Then, to his great relief, he realised Splodge was laughing. Sam began to laugh too. Splodge went over to where a gnome was standing and gently pushed him over. He started to laugh again.

"Ssh," said Sam, who didn't want Hilda and Ernie waking up. "Why are you here?" he asked.

Splodge looked at him as if he had asked about the silliest question going.

"Sauce of the tomato 57," he said.

This was crazy, thought Sam. "You mean tomato ketchup? You have travelled all this way for that?"

"Yes," said Splodge. "I have travelled from Planet Ten Rings to bring home sauce of tomato 57 for my mum as a present for her," he thought hard for a moment, "hello nice to see you day."

"Like a birthday," said Sam.

"What's that?" asked Splodge.

"Oh, you know, the day you were born," Sam said.

"That's it," said Splodge. "A birthday mum present."

"I think you might be in the wrong place," said Sam. "You need a supermarket." He pointed in the direction of the shops. "It's about a kilometre down the road."

Splodge bowed. "Thankyourbits," he said, walking back towards the metal salad washer.

"By the way, what's that?" asked Sam.

"A spaceship," said Splodge,
disappearing inside. The door shut behind
him. Sam waited, not quite knowing what
to do. The spaceship started flashing with
bright colours. There was an alarming
whooshing sound as it started to rise. It
hovered two metres off the ground and
then crashed back down again. Another
loud bang followed, the door slid open,
and Splodge came out bottom first. The
two tufts on the top of his head were
now knotted together.

"Cubut flibnotted," he said.

Broken?" asked Sam.

The little alien nodded. "Whamdangled," he said sadly. "I need to make spaceship see-through."

"Do you mean invisible?" said Sam. "How can you do that?"

Suddenly a light went on in the house, and the curtains were pulled back to reveal Hilda and Ernie, lit up like figures in a toy theatre.

Splodge froze in fright. He had never seen such a scary sight before.

"That's the Bottoms hard?" he said.

"Yes," gulped Sam.

He looked down at Splodge, but to his surprise and alarm he had disappeared. Sam felt very scared, standing there all alone in the garden in the middle of the night in his dressing gown and slippers. How was he going to explain his way out of this one? His legs began to shake. Then to Sam's surprise he heard Splodge's voice.

"Hurry up," he said urgently, "it's invisible time."

"What?" said Sam. He couldn't see Splodge, but could feel something pulling on his pyjama bottoms.

"Hurry up," said Splodge again, "or you'll be whamdangled."

It was too late. The back door opened and there stood Ernie in his gumboots and Hilda in her rollers. She looked more frightening than any alien. She was flashing a torch round the garden. "I think it's that boy out there near the potting shed."

"Where?" said Ernie. "I can't see anything."

"That's because you are a short-sighted nincompoop," she hissed. "If that snivelling, smelly little toerag of a boy is out there he will be in big trouble."

"What are you doing?" said Splodge to Sam. "Now invisible time."

"I can't," said Sam desperately.

It was then that he felt Splodge press something onto his leg and the next thing he knew was that he was completely invisible, except for his slippers, which refused to disappear.

"I think you were seeing things," said Ernie, who just wanted to go back to his warm bed.

"I don't see things," said Hilda flatly. "Put your glasses on, and have a proper look.

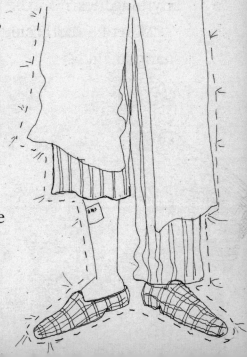

Come on, I don't want to be standing out here all night."

"All right, all right," said Ernie, taking the torch from her. "Oh yes, I think I see something, sweetpea."

"What?" said Hilda, following Ernie.

Sam was frozen to the spot. His slippers seemed to shine out in the moonlight like a neon sign. Hilda and Ernie were moving straight towards him.

"I just…" started Sam.

Ernie looked round. "Did you say anything, dear?"

"Don't be daft, Ernie. Just keep walking," snapped Hilda.

It slowly began to dawn on Sam that he really was invisible and it wasn't his slippers that had caught Ernie's eye, it was the spaceship. Sam started to walk quickly back towards the open back door, his heart thumping so loud that he was sure that even if Hilda couldn't see him, she could hear him. He went into the house, Splodge still clinging on to his leg. Once he was safely inside, Sam shut and locked the back door.

10

Splodge stood in the kitchen tapping his foot. "See now you," he said impatiently to Sam, but all that could be seen of Sam were his dressing gown and slippers. Sam himself was completely invisible.

Sam was enjoying this and he was beginning to think that being invisible might just be the answer to all his problems. He would now be able to escape from the Hardbottoms and get help. That was until he caught sight of himself in the hall mirror. There was nothing to see. How would anyone know he was Sam Ray if he was invisible?

Suddenly there was

a loud noise from behind him. Sam turned round to see Splodge fiddling with a radio. Sam quickly turned it off.

"Flibnotted! Fandangled! Need radio," said Splodge urgently, pulling one of his tufts. "Must understand you better."

Hilda and Ernie were now banging with all their might on the back door.

Sam picked up Splodge and went upstairs to his room and got out his Walkman. Splodge put one earpiece in each tuft, then closed his eyes, folded his arms over his fat little tummy and listened. After a minute or two he started singing at the top of his voice.

"Hip hop it never will stop,

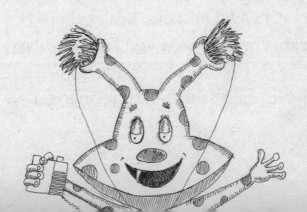

This planet can rock the stars.
Hip hop this never will stop.
We are the men from Mars."

"Not so loud," said Sam desperately to Splodge, who said, "Like the music, dude, it rocks. So tell me, why don't you know how to do visible-invisible? Do you have learning difficulties?"

"No," said Sam, "we humans don't do that." He was beginning to feel a little worried. "What did you put on me in the garden?" he said.

"My one and only patch," said Splodge. "I was going to use it on my spaceship, but when I saw the Bottom hard, and you not doing anything to escape, I did what any other Splodgerdite would have done, helped you out. Because, my H bean, you had gone and forgotten how to go invisible."

"No," said Sam, "I keep telling you we

humans don't do invisible."

"How do you live?" said Splodge with great feeling, as if this was a design fault that should have been mastered years ago. "It must be something awful to be seen all the time."

"It is," said Sam.

"To a Splodgerdite," said Splodge, yawning, "being invisible is like moving leglot. It's just what we do."

"Sorry," said Sam, "you lost me."

Splodge lifted one of his little legs and pointed. "Leglot."

"You mean leg," said Sam.

"Yes," said Splodge. "It's

easy peasy, once you get the handangle of it. Like learning languages." He was now making himself a bed in Hilda's old sock basket. "Next day when the sun comes up to see you," he said sleepily, "I get my spaceship back."

"Will I be visible again tomorrow?" said Sam, but Splodge was fast asleep.

11

Sam woke to find he was quite normal again. He brushed his teeth, washed and got dressed, thinking all the time how wicked it would be if he was really invisible, and went downstairs for breakfast.

He was surprised to see that there were suitcases in the hall, and that Hilda was busy packing tins of food into boxes, which Ernie was taking out to the car. Perhaps, thought Sam, they were leaving and he would finally be able to get away. It was then that he noticed that the back door had a panel missing from it. He was about to ask how that had happened, but the look on Hilda's face told him it wouldn't be a good idea.

"Now listen to me," she said, loading Ernie up with another box. "We are taking you to the seaside for a few days for a holiday."

"I don't want to go, I can't go," said Sam, feeling panicky. "I mean I don't want to leave my house, in case my mum and dad get back and can't find me."

"He's got a point, lambkin," said Ernie resting the box on the edge of the kitchen table. "Anyway, who's going to water my prize pumpkins?"

"You keep out of this, Ernie Hardbottom," said Hilda firmly. "Now you listen to me, young man. Your mum and dad are not coming back ever. The sooner you get that into your head the better."

Sam could feel tears burning at the back of his eyes.

"You should be grateful," said Hilda, picking up the metal salad washer and putting it on top of the box Ernie was carrying, "that we are going to all this trouble just for you."

"There's no need," said Sam desperately. "Why don't you go, and I can stay with a friend?"

Hilda's face twisted into that of a witch.

Sam wasn't going to cry in front of her. He looked again at the metal salad washer. He was sure he had seen it before.

"Where did you get this?" he asked, picking it up.

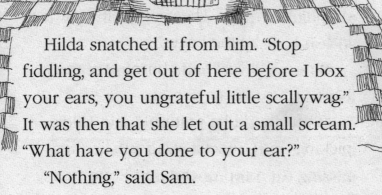

Hilda snatched it from him. "Stop fiddling, and get out of here before I box your ears, you ungrateful little scallywag." It was then that she let out a small scream. "What have you done to your ear?"

"Nothing," said Sam.

"Shouldn't boys have two ears, dearest?" said Ernie.

"Of course they should, peabrain." She pulled Sam over to the mirror. Sure enough one of his ears was invisible, although he could still feel it.

"Perhaps it fell off," said Ernie. "I think we'd better start looking for it, and then take him to the hospital to see if they can stick it back again."

"Shut up, Ernie, and take that box out to the car," said Hilda, looking at Sam carefully. "Are you playing games with me?" she said, reaching out to touch the missing ear. Sam moved away fast.

"I think Ernie's right, we should stay here," said Sam.

"Oh you do, do you?" said Hilda, folding her arms over her ample chest. "Well, I'm not fooled by your little joke. Now get upstairs and pack, and by the way, if you see your missing ear bring it with you."

12

Sam's only comforting
thought was that perhaps it
wasn't a dream, in which case he should
find an alien called Splodge sleeping in the
sewing basket. To his delight and great
relief, there he was, curled up into a ball.

"Good moon to you," said Splodge,
stretching out his little arms.

"We're off, come down here now,"
shouted Hilda.

"Is that the call of the Bottom hard?"
asked Splodge sleepily.

"Look," said Sam, "I don't want to go,
but they are taking me to the seaside and
I can't leave you here all alone."

"I can't leave my spaceship," said
Splodge, "so I suppose this is toodleoo."

"Then I've got bad news," said Sam. "It's
packed in the car that's taking me away.

Hilda thinks it's a salad washer."

Splodge sat up and looked at Sam. "That's a first rate spaceship," he said.

Hilda's voice had got louder and nastier. "If I have to come up and get you, there will be big trouble. Do you hear me, boy?"

Without another word Splodge got up, made his way over to the rucksack and climbed in. "The one good thing is that you're visible again," he said, making himself comfortable.

"Apart from one ear," said Sam, picking up his rucksack.

"What's an ear between aliens?" said Splodge.

The Ford Cortina was packed to bursting. Ernie was so small that he had to sit on three cushions before he could see over the wheel. Sam wondered why Hilda didn't drive, as she was the one that gave all the instructions.

"You are going too fast, keep over to the left, no you shouldn't be in that gear."

All Ernie would say was a feeble, "Yes dear, no dear."

It took the best part of a day to get Skipton-on-Sea and when they finally arrived, smoke was coming out of the bonnet of the car. It came to a grinding halt outside a dismal-looking bungalow that smelt of damp and was colder inside than it was out. Why anyone would come here for a holiday was beyond Sam. His heart sank.

"This will do very nicely," said Hilda.

"Well," said Ernie, "the sea air must agree with our Sam because look, sweetpea, his ear is back again."

"Of course it is," snapped Hilda. "It was only that smelly little toerag's idea of a joke and I don't laugh that easily."

"No," said Ernie, "no, you don't."

13

It was hard to imagine a more miserable and isolated place. Even when tea was made and the lights turned on it had the feeling of being at the end of the world, and there was no way back.

Sam's room was smaller than the last one, and worst of all, the walls seemed to be made of paper. He could hear every word of what Hilda and Ernie had to say and none of it was good. Finally he could hear Hilda snoring, and he knew he was safe to look in his rucksack. He wanted to make sure he hadn't gone completely mad that morning imagining an alien, and a spaceship that looked like a salad washer. It was the only thing that had given him hope, as they drove farther and farther away from his home, from all that he knew and loved.

Sam emptied his rucksack carefully. There was no Splodge. He must have imagined it. He looked again. There were only the few things he had packed this morning. He turned it inside out. Tears started to roll down his face. He should have run away before they kidnapped him. Now Sam was lost just like his mum and dad.

He was lying in bed wondering, if he ran away, would he be able to find his way back, when the bedroom door opened all by itself.

Sam sat up in bed and flashed his torch. There, slowly making its way across the floor, without anyone helping it, was a bottle of tomato ketchup.

It came to a stop, and then Sam heard the padding of little feet and saw a plate of finger-size sandwiches wobbling in the air. They tottered one way, then another. Sam shone his torch on to the plate. A small voice said, "Stop it, I can't see."

"Is that you, Splodge?" said Sam hopefully.

"Who else," said Splodge, becoming visible again, with the plate of sandwiches in his hands. Sam had never been so pleased to see an alien before.

"These," said Splodge proudly, "are for you. Sandwiches of tomato ketchup and pea butter with nut."

Sam was so hungry that he ate them all down. They tasted great.

"Good news," said Splodge, "I have found my spaceship. Bad bit, wet inside."

"That's because Hilda thinks it's a salad washer," said Sam.

"It's a Viszler Junior Space Carrier," said

Splodge, sounding offended, "and that monster alien thinks it's a salad washer, whatever that may be."

"It's something you put lettuce in and then you whizz it around and hey presto you have clean lettuce," said Sam, finishing the last of the sandwiches.

"Or hay pisboo you have a broken spaceship," said Splodge.

"I'm sorry," said Sam.

Splodge didn't look up. He was busy, comforting himself by sucking the tomato ketchup out of the bottle.

For the first time since coming to stay with the Hardbottoms, Sam didn't feel alone. He sat on the bed with Splodge, looking out of the window. The moon looked like a big balloon that had come to rest on the garden wall.

Sam told Splodge about his parents' disastrous trip and how everyone thought they were dead and lost in space.

Splodge tutted. "I shouldn't think so, they most probably got stuck inside a grotter. Has anybody gone and looked?"

"What's that?" asked Sam.

"Surely you know what a grotter is," said Splodge.

"No I don't," said Sam. "I haven't a clue, what is it?"

Splodge looked worried. "Don't you learn anything at school then?"

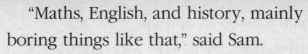

"Maths, English, and history, mainly boring things like that," said Sam.

"Not about the planets, and the stars, and space dragons?" said Splodge. "Or how to look after a grotter, and what to do if an orgback turns up?"

"No," said Sam, who thought he would much rather learn about space than William the Conqueror.

"Grotters," continued Splodge, "are black as space and hard to see. They have huge tum tums and float about with their mouths wide open feeding on metricels of light, gaggerling up whatever gets in their way."

Sam looked at Splodge, still not understanding what he was talking about.

"Planet Ten Rings," explained Splodge, "is milacue. So we look after the grotters and they look after us. Keep the orgbacks away, for a start."

"What are they?" said Sam.

"Humungous space monsters that can gaggerly up whole stars," said Splodge.

"Why don't you think an orgback swallowed the Star Shuttle then?" said Sam.

"Not possible, they live deep in space and we hardly ever see them. They wouldn't be bothered with a smidger of a thing like a spaceship. It wouldn't be worth munching."

"Would a Star Shuttle be all right inside a grotter or would that be the end of it?" asked Sam anxiously.

"More likely to make a grotter tum feel all wobbly and wonky," said Splodge. "I need to get a message home to my mum and dad. Then I would be able to tell them about the Star Shuttle."

But the problem was, how were they going to do that, now Splodge's spaceship was broken.

15

The morning did not bring with it a cheerful picture of holiday bliss. Thin drizzle fell and Sam could not see the sea because of a cement wall that blocked out the view. All the neighbouring bungalows were boarded up.

Hilda was busy trying to sort out the kitchen. "Did you get up in the night and take some food?" she said in a menacing voice.

"No," said Sam.

"Well, there are breadcrumbs where breadcrumbs shouldn't be," said Hilda.

"Perhaps there's mice," said Sam.

Hilda picked up the broom and shook it at Sam. "I don't want any more of your cheek, you little toerag. Go out and play."

"It's raining," said Sam.

"Out!" shouted Hilda.

Sam went out into the back yard. You couldn't call it a garden. It had high walls and crazy paving, and looked more like a prison yard. In it were two broken garden chairs, a washing line with a mouldy dishcloth hanging from it, and a pot with some tired plastic flowers sticking out of it.

Ernie was in the tiny shed at the back, fiddling about with wires.

"What are you doing?" asked Sam.

Ernie nearly jumped out of his skin. "Nothing, dear, nothing," he said. "Oh, it's you. What do you want?"

"It's raining," said Sam.

"Oh all right, you can stay here, but don't fiddle," said Ernie.

"What's that?" asked Sam, pointing to a funny-looking machine.

"It's a citizen's band radio," said Ernie, beaming with pride as he showed Sam how it worked. "It's not like your everyday radio. Before I retired I used to

drive long distance lorries, and this is how
we talked to each other. We all had
different names." Ernie blushed and said,
"I was called Tiger Raw. Sometimes if I
was lucky, I would be able to pick up
signals on it from as far away as Russia
and beyond. Isn't she beautiful!"

"Could it send messages into space?"
asked Sam eagerly.

"I don't rightly know," said Ernie,
scratching the top of his head. "That's a

mighty long way away, isn't it. I mean, it's farther than Russia."

"Only a little bit," said Sam.

"Anyway, I've just bought a bigger receiver," said Ernie, "but I'm having trouble wiring it up. The instructions seem to be written in double Dutch," he said sadly, looking at the manual.

"Ernie, where are you?" shouted Hilda.

"Out here, sweetpea," called Ernie.

"What are you doing?"

"Nothing, dearest, just fiddling," said Ernie.

"Stop it right now," shouted Hilda, "and come in here and help me make pea soup. And you too," Hilda shouted at Sam.

An awful smell of overcooked vegetables greeted them as they walked into the kitchen.

"I want you to stir this," said Hilda, showing Sam a pot of smelly, slimy green liquid. "Don't let it stick to the bottom. That soup is going to have to last us a week."

Sam sighed, and did as he was told. It was then that he realised both his hands were going invisible.

"Hilda," said Ernie, staring at Sam, "do you think boys fade away when they are unhappy?"

"What gibberish are you talking now, Ernie?" said Hilda.

"Sam's hands. They've gone and vanished," said Ernie.

Hilda turned on Sam. "You are doing this on purpose, aren't you, you ungrateful boy, and after all the trouble that we've gone to!"

"I just want to go home," said Sam bravely. "I shouldn't be here."

"He's got a point, dearest," said Ernie.

Hilda looked more frightening than an old flesh-eating dinosaur, all red and furious. "You keep out of this, you peabrain," she snapped, towering over Sam. "You'd better stay in your room until you learn not to play any more of these jokes, or you'll be sorry you were ever born."

16

Splodge was on the bed, listening to Sam's Walkman, and finishing off the last of the tomato ketchup.

"The good news," said Sam, sitting down next to him, "is that Ernie has a radio and a powerful receiver which he can't work. It just might get a message back to your planet. The bad news is, I'm grounded until my hands become visible again."

"It's going to be a long time then," said Splodge.

Sam was slowly fading away. By teatime he was completely invisible. All that could be seen of him were his clothes.

"I don't think I should have stuck that patch on you, " said Splodge anxiously. "It was meant for spacecraft, not for H beans."

"Stop worrying," said Sam. "Look, last time I came back, so why wouldn't it happen again?"

Splodge tried explaining about invisibility, but it was no use, Sam was far too excited, working out the best combination for frightening the pants off Hilda Hardbottom.

"Hi," he said calmly, walking into the kitchen for tea. "I am so hungry I am almost fading away."

Ernie and Hilda nearly jumped out of their skins when they saw a cap and a pair of trousers coming towards them.

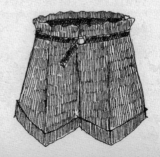

"I don't think this is right, dearest," said Ernie, dropping the newspaper. "Shouldn't we be able to see him?"

"Of course we should," said Hilda shakily.

"I think it might be best to take him home, and get a doctor to have a look at him," said Ernie.

"What do you think would happen, you ninny, if we went home with an invisible boy?" said Hilda,

"I don't know, sweetpea," said Ernie.

Hilda sat down at the kitchen table. She was really worried. This wasn't in her grand plan. In fact she could be accused of causing Sam's disappearance. Then they would be in deep trouble. Hilda couldn't allow her plan to go wrong, not now when she was so close to getting what she wanted. Maureen Cook from Dream Maker Tours had said it was only a matter of her seeing Sam, then the money would be as good as theirs.

"Remember the ear, sweetpea, it came back," said Ernie, trying to sound encouraging.

Hilda filled their bowls with green slimy pea soup.

"Eat up," she said, putting on her TV face, "we don't want you fading away altogether now, do we."

Sam took off his cap and put it on the table. Hilda jumped back. There was now nothing to show that Sam was sitting in his seat, except a spoon playing with the slimy soup.

"I don't much like pea soup," said Sam, who was enjoying seeing Hilda squirm.

"What do you like?" said Hilda nervously. "You can have anything you want as long as it helps make you visible again."

So Sam gave her a long list, starting with twelve small bottles of tomato ketchup.

17

That night Hilda couldn't sleep. She was walking up and down in the lounge when a picture came off the wall right in front of her, and a china dog started to move across the mantelpiece. Sam was having fun.

"Is that you, Sam?" she said in a shaky voice. Sam didn't answer. Splodge, who was also invisible, was tickling her leg. She let out a scream and Ernie came in, yawning. What he saw made his legs wobbly with fright. A chair was floating round the room.

"That's not right," said Ernie, "I mean, chairs don't do that, do they?"

The chair dropped to the ground with a thud.

"Of course they don't, you ninny," Hilda said trembling.

"You know, sweetpea," said Ernie, "I think this place might be haunted. I just felt a rush of cold air." The lounge door closed with a bang.

Hilda recovered herself. "Of course it's not haunted," she snapped, picking up a cushion and hitting out at thin air. "Take that, you little toerag," she shouted. But Sam and Splodge had left, and were safely out of the way in the shed.

"I like being invisible," said Sam. "The only drawback is that it's chilly without your clothes on."

"Pish bosh, you're supposed to come and go, not stay like that all the time," said Splodge. "The sooner we get a message home the better."

The CB radio was not working that well, mainly because it had been wired to the receiver the wrong way. It took

Splodge some time to get it sorted out.

"Come on," said Sam, "I'm getting chilly out here."

"Well go back to the monster grotto then," said Splodge, "and make us something to fill up gurgling tummy."

The radio was now making strange noises and Splodge kept moving the knobs and listening. Then he started speaking in a language that Sam couldn't understand.

"Χαλλινγ Πλανεντ τεν ρινγσ"

Sam walked back towards the bungalow. The lounge looked as if a giant hippo had had hysterics. Hilda had finally gone to bed exhausted, and was snoring like a battleship attacking her enemy.

The great thing about being invisible, thought Sam, opening the fridge and looking inside, is that I don't feel frightened any more. I have some power and that is a truly wicked feeling. He poured out all the milk there was into two glasses, made a pile of peanut butter sandwiches and found the last bottle of tomato ketchup.

"I've got message home," said Splodge, becoming visible again. "They've heard of a sick grotter, in fact it's caused quite a hollerburluke. Something is definitely stuck inside it. They're on their way out to it. Also my mum says not to worry and sends you her toodle hyes."

"Oh that's wonderful," said Sam.
"So what will happen now?"

"Mum and Dad want to say hi and talk
to me again tomorrow. Also I've got to tell
them about the invisible problem,"
mumbled Splodge. "I'm sure my dad
and mum can think of something."

18

The bungalow was unusually quiet the next morning. Hilda had taken the car into the village to do some shopping, and Ernie was in the shed, playing with his radio. To his delight it was working better than it had ever done before, picking up some very strange sounds, "Χαλλινγ σπλογε σπαχε σηυττλε ρχοϖερεδ αλλ ον βοαρδ αρε σαφε."

Sam and Splodge spent the best part of the morning in the lounge. Sam was still invisible, but today he was dressed. It was too chilly to walk about without your clothes on. They sat together on the beaten up

sofa, eating cereal out of the packet, watching whatever they wanted on TV.

Ernie, who had been left with strict instructions not to let Sam out of his sight, kept coming in from the shed, and saying, "You all right then?" On one of these visits he was sure he saw a green spotty little fellow sitting next to Sam, but then again he might just be seeing things, he hadn't got his glasses on, and the next time he looked it had gone.

About two o'clock the phone rang. Ernie picked it up. It was Maureen Cook from Dream Maker Tours. She couldn't have sounded more helpful, and said she would be coming down to see Sam tomorrow, to talk about his future.

"That will be nice," said Ernie, putting down the phone and telling Sam what she had just said.

"Do you think she will recognise me?" asked Sam.

"Oh dear," said Ernie. "Oh dear, I forgot you were invisible."

Hilda was not in a good mood when she arrived home at teatime, weighed down by shopping bags. Her mood was not improved one little bit when Ernie told her about Maureen Cook. She started rumbling like an old boiler ready to burst.

"You are worse than hopeless, you peabrain," she said to Ernie, who was looking very sheepish. "What are we going to show her, an invisible boy?"

"Perhaps," said Sam, "if you were kind to me, I might become visible again."

"It's worth a try," said Ernie in a small shaky voice.

Hilda said nothing, but banged and thumped round the kitchen unpacking the shopping.

"Oh that looks nice, sweetpea," said Ernie, seeing all the things Sam had asked for, including the twelve bottles of tomato ketchup.

"Well, none of it's for you," she snapped at Ernie. "It isn't you that's invisible, more's the pity." She handed Sam a bag. "Put these on," she ordered.

In it were a woolly balaclava, a pair of multi-coloured gloves, a cheap pair of dark glasses, and as the finishing touch, a pair of plastic joke lips.

"What are these for?" said Sam, laughing.

"This isn't funny," said Hilda. "Just do as I say."

When he saw himself in the hall mirror he couldn't stop laughing. Oh, now he really did look scary, as if he were about to rob a bank. Roll on tomorrow, he thought. How was Hilda going to get out of this mess?

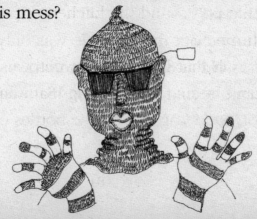

19

The reason, Splodge said, that Splodgerdites adored tomato ketchup was simple. It was the sauce of their good looks, it kept them young, healthy, and wise. Also, growing tomatoes was unheard of on Planet Ten Rings. It was only on earth that the tomato could be transformed into the right stuff for aliens.

"Have you been here lots of times, then?" asked Sam.

Splodge looked down at his toes. "No," he said, "I have only been here once before with my dad, and it was a short sort of visit."

It turned out that Splodge was only about as old as Sam, and that this was the first time he had travelled on his own to earth.

"I thought I would get my mum a present," said Splodge sadly, "but it all went a bit starshaped. I am only a junior space flyer, I start my AST course next year."

"What's that?" asked Sam.

"Advanced Space Travel," said Splodge. "That's when we learn everything to do with space and all the other things like grotters and orgbacks."

Sam didn't like to ask, he had a nasty feeling he already knew the answer.

"Have you ever used one of those invisible patches before?" he said.

"No," said Splodge.

"Do you know what happens when one of those patches is put on a boy like me?" asked Sam.

"No," said Splodge, looking a little shamefaced. "They are only to be used when everything is whamdangled."

Sam was beginning to feel panicky. It was one thing to be invisible for a few

days, but not forever. What if his parents
came back? How would they know it was
Sam if they couldn't see him?

"Will I ever be visible again?" asked
Sam anxiously.

"Need to speak to Dad," said Splodge.
"I'm sure someone on Ten Rings will
know what to do."

But it was proving to be
quite difficult to get a message home.
Ernie had been fiddling again with the
radio and it took Splodge ages to pick up
a signal, and then he could hardly hear
what they were saying, except for the odd
word like σουνδ σηυττλε σαφε.

"We'll have to try again tomorrow," said Sam, seeing the look on Splodge's face. He was tired and his bright green skin was losing its shine.

"Pish bosh, I want to go home," he said sadly. "I miss my mum."

"I know," said Sam. He took Splodge back to the house, gave him a bottle of tomato ketchup and tucked him up in bed.

"So do I," said Sam quietly. "I miss Mum and Dad very much indeed."

20

The next day the Hardbottoms were up early, cleaning and tidying the bungalow.

Hilda put on her smiling face that she kept at the bottom of an old make-up bag and only used for special occasions. Ernie put on his one and only suit. The tea had been set out on a tray in the lounge, and the curtains were drawn. Hilda had put

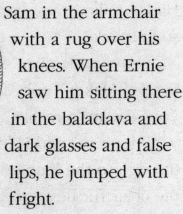

Sam in the armchair with a rug over his knees. When Ernie saw him sitting there in the balaclava and dark glasses and false lips, he jumped with fright.

"Hilda," he said, "there's a strange man sitting in the armchair.

He wasn't there a moment ago. Did you let him in? He looks very scary!"

"That, you peabrain, is Sam," said Hilda.

When Maureen Cook arrived she was rather taken aback by the Hardbottoms' idea of a holiday. The bungalow was seedy, and smelt damp.

"You could have taken yourselves somewhere nice and hot," she said. "We would happily have paid."

"Didn't want to look too greedy," said Hilda, smiling. "Not until all this is settled, so to speak."

"Please remember," said Maureen, "Dream Maker Tours are here to make your dreams a reality."

"I hope so," said Hilda, taking Maureen through to the lounge, and placing her in the chair furthest away from Sam. Hilda handed her a cup of tea and a piece of cake, talking all the time, like a car alarm that wouldn't stop, about how much they cared for Sam and how he enjoyed sitting in the dark wearing a balaclava.

"It makes him feel protected from the outside world. Grief," said Hilda, "can do strange things to one."

"Please Mrs Hardbottom," said Maureen, "will you let me speak. Are you feeling all right, Sam?" she asked.

"As I said," interrupted Hilda, "Sam is a bit shy."

Sam nodded and mumbled, "I'm OK."

"Do you like it here?" Maureen started.

Hilda interrupted again. "These questions aren't too strenuous, are they?" she said, sounding concerned. "It's just that we care so much for the boy, and want to protect him. After all, I'm not called the Nation's Favourite Neighbour for nothing."

"Quite so," said Maureen, bringing a picture of Sam out of her briefcase, and going over to the window to draw back the curtains. "I would like to see your face,

Sam, if you don't mind."

"I do mind," said Hilda, rushing past her and standing in front of the window. "He has been through an awful lot, why does he have to answer these questions? Isn't it enough that he's here?"

"I am just doing my job, Mrs Hardbottom," said Maureen wearily. This wasn't going to plan. She had hoped to have all this sorted out in no time at all.

"Treacle toffee," said Hilda, holding out a sweet tin. "I made it myself."

Maureen smiled weakly. "Well, one piece if you insist, then I must ask Sam these questions."

Sam watched the look of horror spread over Maureen Cook's face as her jaws slowly stuck together and she was unable to say another word.

Hilda took her back to the chair farthest away from Sam.

"Shall we talk about the money?" said Hilda, smiling charmingly.

At that moment Ernie came into the room. "Wonderful news, sweetpea," he said. "The Star shuttle has made contact with Earth. I just heard it on my CB radio. It looks like Mr and Mrs Ray will be coming home after all."

"Hooray!" shouted Sam, sending the false pair of lips shooting across the room.

Maureen looked startled and Sam put his gloved hand across his mouth and said, "It's the best bit of news ever."

21

Maureen Cook had written out a cheque to cover their holiday expenses.

"Is that all?" said Hilda, seeing how little she had been given.

But Maureen was now running towards her car, still unable to speak, a hanky held over her mouth.

"Wait a minute, come back," shouted Hilda.

It was too late. Maureen sped off down the road at top speed.

"It's all your fault," Hilda screamed at Ernie. "If you hadn't come charging in like that, we would have been given loads of money."

Hilda marched like an invading army into the shed. She got hold of the CB radio, and lifted it high above her head.

"Don't do that!" shouted Ernie and Sam together. It was too late. Hilda threw it to the ground.

"I think," said Ernie sadly, "you've gone and broken it."

"I hope so," said Hilda. "If you had half a brain, you would have seen what I was trying to do instead of mucking up all my plans."

Hilda went back into the kitchen followed by Sam. All that could be seen of him now was a pair of dark glasses.

"You wretched boy, none of this would have happened if you hadn't gone invisible," yelled Hilda. "Well, you can stop playing games. I haven't come this far for you to ruin everything. You are going to become visible again and tell your mum and dad you had a lovely time with us.

Do you hear me?"

Sam, who had long lost his fear of Hilda, said calmly, "I won't. I will tell them the truth, that you are a mean, nasty two-faced witch."

Hilda grabbed a broom. "What did you call me?" she shouted, bringing it down with a nasty crack on the sunglasses, which fell broken to the floor.

At that moment Splodge walked into the room, quite visible.

"I agree," he said.

Hilda dropped her broom and scrambled up on the table as fast as her tubby legs would let her. Splodge went over to where the broken glasses lay, and picked them up.

"You," said Splodge, "should be boggled."

Hilda started screaming at the top of her voice.

Ernie came in holding his smashed radio.

"Look!" yelled Hilda, pointing at Splodge. "It's a monster, a rat, an alien. Don't stand there, do something!"

If Ernie wasn't mistaken, this was the same little fellow that he had seen sitting with Sam the other day on the sofa.

"Well, what are you waiting for? I think that creature has murdered Sam!" said Hilda "Look at the smashed glasses."

Ernie said nothing. He had seen many frightening things in his life, though sadly none of them as frightening as his wife when she was in one of her moods.

"I can't see what all the fuss is about," said Sam, invisible from the other side of the room. "That's my friend Splodge, from Planet Ten Rings, and he's not best pleased that you have ruined his spaceship by filling it with water."

Hilda went white with fright. "Do something, Ernie," she pleaded.

For the first time since he had married Hilda, way back in the dark ages, Ernie felt brave. If a boy and a little alien could stand up to her, so could he.

"No, I won't," he said firmly. "You have gone too far this time, Hilda. I should have had the courage to stop you, but I didn't – more's the pity."

Splodge stepped forward. "You are a cruel and mean hard bottom, and you give earth H beans a bad name," he said, holding his little hands out before him. Bright green rays came out of his fingertips. Hilda's face went a horrid pink and then became covered in tiny green spots.

"Nice one," said Sam.

Hilda quickly climbed down off the table, ran into the hall, grabbed her coat and hat, stuffed the cheque into her handbag and ran out of the front door and down the street as fast as her stumpy legs would carry her.

22

On the TV that night, every programme was about the Star Shuttle's miraculous return to earth. Experts were talking about black holes and all sort of other theories to explain how a spaceship could go missing for so long. No one mentioned grotters or a small planet called Ten Rings.

Splodge had been spending the evening trying to wire the radio up to his spaceship in the hope of getting a message home, but it wasn't working. Ernie was out in the back yard with the receiver.

"Try it now," said Ernie.

There were a few beeping noises and then nothing.

"Pish bosh, it's hopeless," said Splodge sadly. "We are truly boggled."

"Often when things don't work," said Sam "my dad gives them a little tap. He says it helps them wake up."

"Go on then," said Splodge.

Sam tapped the top of the spaceship. Nothing happened.

"Well," said Splodge, "it doesn't work."

But that was as far as he got. The spaceship suddenly lit up. Sparks of rainbow colour came shooting out of it, lighting up the drab back yard.

"OW!" said Sam.

Then they all heard

Τηισ ισ πλανεντ τεν Ρινγσ Χαλλινγ Σπλοδγε

"That's my dad!" shouted Splodge.
"That's my dad!"

It was a much larger spacecraft that
landed in the back yard that night, and
Splodge's parents were thrilled to see their
son.

"This is Sam," said Splodge, looking
down at his toes. Sam held out the arm of
his old jumper.

"Oh dear," said Splodge's dad. "What
have you done, junior?"

"He was trying to protect me," said Sam.

"He didn't realise I couldn't go invisible."

"Sorry, Dad," said Splodge.

His dad smiled a kind smile. "Well, we'd better put it right."

He held out his hands and a blue light flashed around Sam. The next thing, there he was, visible again.

"Thank you," said Sam. "Oh, it's great to be seen again."

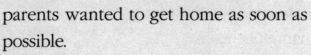

Ernie offered to make them tea, but Splodge's parents wanted to get home as soon as possible.

"Wait a minute, I can't go without Mum's present," said Splodge.

He rushed back into the bungalow and brought out twelve bottles of tomato ketchup.

"These are for you, Mum," said Splodge.

She gave him a hug, then thanked Sam for looking after him so well. "He's a bit young to be doing this," she said, waving goodbye. Sam wanted to thank Splodge's parents for helping him find his mum and dad, but there was no time. He was interrupted by the noise of police cars screeching down the road. Splodge just had time to wave before the doors of the spaceship closed behind him. Then there was a whirling noise and in a shower of lights and glitter they were gone.

The police were now knocking loudly on the front door. "Mr and Mrs Hardbottom," they shouted, "open up in the name of the law."

23

It was the best homecoming ever. Mum and Dad were over the moon to see their beloved boy. They couldn't have been more proud of Sam, and how well he had coped under such appalling circumstances. It was hard to believe that Hilda could have turned out to be so cruel and horrible.

It had been Maureen Cook who had alerted the police. They had arrived just in time to see sparks coming from behind the garden wall.

They had driven Sam home in style to his parents, the blue lights flashing all the way to 2 Plunket Road.

Ernie had been taken away for questioning, while Hilda was caught trying to get on a flight for Majorca. It was her pink face with its green spots that had given her away.

Mr and Mrs Hardbottom were both charged with abduction and trying to take money under false pretences.

The Comet

The neighbour from hell

Hilda had at last found the fame she had been looking for. Her picture appeared on every newspaper, with the caption "The neighbour from hell." She was sent to prison. Ernie was let off with a caution. The judge felt that if he hadn't been so frightened of his wife he wouldn't have gone along with her plan.

Mum and Dad felt relieved that it was all over, and they were just happy to be back on earth with Sam.

The funny thing was they had no memory at all of what happened to them, except of falling asleep on the homeward journey and waking up again as they were landing. Everyone on board had been most surprised to find out that anything had been wrong, or that they had been missing for so long. Even the officials at Houston agreed that the space shuttle disappearance was a mystery.

"It's like it became invisible," said one Houston scientist.

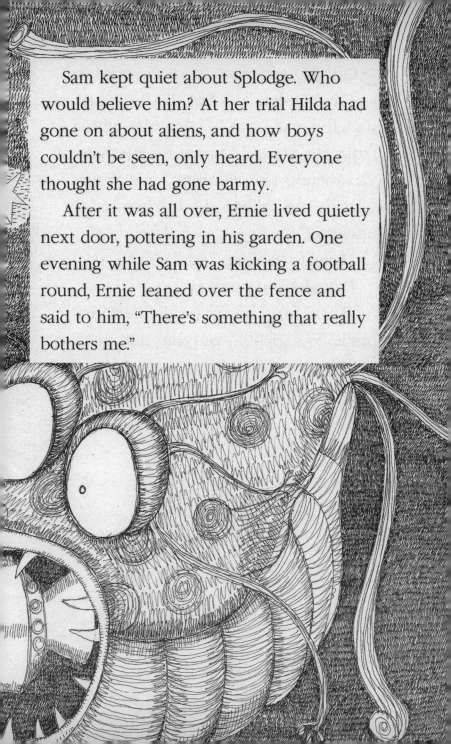

Sam kept quiet about Splodge. Who would believe him? At her trial Hilda had gone on about aliens, and how boys couldn't be seen, only heard. Everyone thought she had gone barmy.

After it was all over, Ernie lived quietly next door, pottering in his garden. One evening while Sam was kicking a football round, Ernie leaned over the fence and said to him, "There's something that really bothers me."

"What?" said Sam.

"That little fellow Splodge, he asked me something as I was helping him with the radio. He said did I know the meaning of 57 varieties? Do you think," said Ernie, "that he was talking about space and the universe?"

"Tomato ketchup," said Sam.

Ernie looked puzzled.

"That's what it says on the ketchup bottle, 57 varieties," said Sam, and they both burst out laughing.

The Boy with the
Magic Numbers

ALSO BY SALLY GARDNER

The Boy who could Fly
The Boy with the Lightning Feet
The Smallest Girl Ever
The Strongest Girl in the World

For younger readers
A Book of Princesses
Fairy Catalogue
Fairy Shopping
The Glass Heart
Playtime Rhymes
The Real Fairy Storybook (text by Georgie Adams)

For older readers
I, Coriander

The Boy with the
Magic Numbers

Sally Gardner

Orion
Children's Books

to a star
Elena Salvoni
love Sally

1

The present that Dad had left for Billy
Pickles was placed under the note that he
had stuck to his barber's shop mirror. It said
simply, "My number came up and it wasn't
the right one. Sorry."

The present was a money-box shaped
like the top half of a man. It had a large
smiley face and its two hands were folded
over its chubby tummy. Billy wondered
where the money went in. He couldn't see
a slot. It said on the box BATTERIES NOT
INCLUDED.

Mum and Billy stood together in the gathering gloom of the barber's shop. They looked at the money-box for a long time, hoping that it might tell them why Dad had gone, and where.

Neither of them spoke and neither of them turned on the lights. They were both looking for clues in the darkness, but everything was just as it had always been. There were the barber's chairs standing in a row, the TV fish tank with its tropical fish swimming aimlessly round and round, the wall covered with framed pictures of Italy and Mighty Mamma.

It was Billy who noticed that Dad's favourite signed photograph was missing. When Mum saw the gap on the wall she let out a little gasp. Dad had taken with him the picture of his hero, the King of Swing, Mr Frank Sinatra.

Billy walked over to the CD player and turned it on. Immediately, Frank Sinatra

sang out loud and clear, full of energy and hope:

"New York, New York!"

"I think your dad's gone for good this time, Billy," Mum said softly, turning the music off.

Billy picked up his present and said, "Where do you put the money in?"

"I'm not sure, love," said Mum. "We'll have a proper look at it when we get home. I think we both need a nice cup of tea."

2

Dad's leaving had the same effect as a stone when it is thrown into a pond. The ripples in the water spread out, upsetting everything. Under the stairs, Mum discovered twenty-seven boxes of unopened bills. Before she could do anything about them, the bailiffs turned up and took away the car and the TV.

"Why are they doing that?" asked Billy.

"Your dad liked what he called a flutter on the horses. He bet more money than he had," said Mum. She sighed. "The bailiffs are taking away whatever's valuable so that they can get some of the money back again."

Over the next few months, nearly all the furniture disappeared and Billy and Mum had to put their little house on the market. They moved into rented rooms just above the barber's shop.

Mum was not going to be defeated. It wasn't the first time Dad had gone off without saying a word. But this time it had the feeling of being final. She left her job to take over Dad's barber's shop and put a new notice in the window. It said 'Lily's Unisex Haircuts'.

Dad's regular customers were disappointed not to have Tony cutting their hair and giving them the latest racing tips. They liked listening to Tony's tales. "He'll be back," they said, but when Mum told them just how much Dad owed they had nothing more to say.

Mum's lady customers weren't keen on having their hair done in a barber's chair, so keeping it all going took the roses out of Mum's cheeks.

Billy put the money-box on his window-sill. He would look at it, wondering what it would do if it worked. The instructions said it took Double B batteries and that it only

9

accepted American dimes. No one in their
small town had ever heard of Double B
batteries and Billy hadn't a penny, let alone
a dime.

"Never mind, love," said Mum. "It was
the thought that counted."

So Dad's thought stayed on Billy's
window-sill, reminding him of all he had
lost.

3

What Billy missed most about his dad was the stories he told of Italy and Mighty Mamma. Dad, who had been christened Antonio Piccoloni, had been the baby of the family. His older brother, Santo, had left home by the time he was born.

"You see, Billy," Dad would laugh, "I wanted Mamma all for myself."

His childhood was a golden time when he dreamed of owning a chain of barbers' shops all over the world. When he grew up, he came to England to make his dream come true. This was how he met Lily, Billy's mum, at a hairdressers' convention in Harrogate.

"The only beautiful woman outside Italy, so what could I do?" And as he said this, he would lift his shoulders and put on a sad face like a clown. "I had to stay and

become Tony Pickles."

This always made Billy laugh.

"One day, Billy, when my number comes up, you and me are going to travel. We will visit Mighty Mamma and go see my brother Santo's ice cream café in New York. What you say?"

Billy couldn't wait. Although Dad had never been to New York, his stories of the city were better than fairy tales. New York, according to Dad, was like a magical castle built out of skyscrapers, where in the streets far below the yellow taxi dragons did battle. It was a place where a dreamer could become a king.

About a month after Dad had gone, a postcard arrived. It had a picture of the Statue of Liberty on it and it said

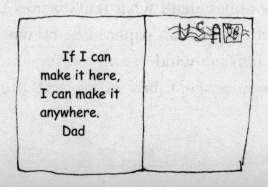

If I can make it here, I can make it anywhere.
Dad

Mum stuck it in the gap where the picture of Frank Sinatra had been.

Billy tried not to think about his dad, but it was hard when there was so much he wanted to ask him. All the questions began with a why. Why did he go off like that without saying a word? Why had he left Mum? Why had he left everything in such a mess?

The trouble was, Billy didn't know how to get hold of Dad to ask him.

"New York's a big place, Billy," said Mum.

"He might be at Uncle Santo's," said Billy hopefully. Mum asked International Directory Enquiries for their help to find the number, but Santo's ice cream café in New York wasn't listed.

"Maybe he'll write soon," said Mum.

Paper kites, that's what Dad's stories were. No more than paper kites, blown away with the wind.

Billy now spent most of his time after

school helping Mum in the barber's shop.
They were a team. Mum hadn't enough
money to change it into a proper
hairdressing salon, but at least the old
customers hadn't left her, and because she
was so good she soon had some new ones.

Dad's customers missed his horse-racing
tips, but Mum had another trick up her
sleeve. Her mother had taught her to read
the future in the tea leaves. It was an art
form, she told Billy.

Mum wasn't sure how good she was at
it but the customers weren't complaining.
There was now a steady flow of people
coming and going all day.

"Better make me look extra smart tonight, Lily," the ladies would say, "if you're right about that tall handsome man."

In the evening Billy would sit with Mum and neatly write down all the money she had made in a little cash book.

"Oh, Billy boy, you make those numbers look magical!" said Mum with pride.

Yet in spite of all Mum's hard work, they were unable to do more than keep their heads above water.

Mum had a little feeling that something was about to change. She'd seen it in the tea leaves. But neither she nor Billy could have imagined just how much, nor that it would have something to do with Mighty Mamma and the money-box.

4

A letter from Dad had arrived at the beginning of the Easter holidays. In it was a small cheque for Mum and a ticket to New York for Billy. Dad wanted him to come out and stay so that he could meet Mighty Mamma. She was coming over from Italy for the seventieth birthday party that Uncle Santo was giving for her.

Billy was so excited. He had never travelled further than Lytham St Anne's. This would be an adventure.

"You won't be upset if I go, Mum?" said Billy, looking at his mum's pale face.

"No," said Mum. "I think it's a good idea if Dad answers all your why questions himself."

A week later Billy was sitting on a plane flying to the other side of the world, all by himself. He was seated next to a plump

boy about his own age, dressed in school uniform.

"Hi," said the boy. "I'm Walter Minks Junior."

"I'm Billy Pickles," said Billy, trying to figure out how you worked the video.

Walter leant over to help.

"Are you flying on your own too?" said Billy.

"Yes, I fly all the time. I go to boarding school in Sussex and come home to the States every holiday."

Billy and Walter got on well, and talking

and playing cards made the journey go by faster.

"Do you live in New York?" asked Billy.

"Yep. Nope. I spend half the holidays with my dad in New York and the other half with my mum in Hollywood," said Walter.

Billy showed him the address Dad had sent him.

"You're not that far away from my dad," said Walter. "Look, why don't I give you my number and I'll take yours, and maybe we can meet up?"

"I'd like that," said Billy.

An air steward saw the two boys through immigration and out into a wave of waiting people. It seemed to Billy that he had landed on another planet. Everything was whirling around him. He couldn't see Dad anywhere.

"Who's meeting you boys?" asked the steward.

"My driver," said Walter.

"My dad," said Billy with pride.

A very smart man stepped forward.

"That's him," said Walter. "Hope to see you again, Billy." And he faded into the crowd.

Billy stood there, feeling suddenly very alone and wondering where his dad could be. The steward said kindly, "Don't worry, Billy. The traffic out of New York can be bad. I'm sure your dad will be here soon."

"Billy!" Someone was shouting. "Billy!"

Billy looked round, but he couldn't see anyone he knew. Then the crowds parted and before him stood a small elderly lady not much taller than himself. She had a pretty face and dark brown eyes.

"Billy Pickles! Oh, how good to see you! I knew it was you. You look just like your nonno, my late husband Alfredo." She gave Billy two kisses on each cheek.

Billy looked startled.

"You don't know who I am? I am Mighty

Mamma, your nonna, your grandmother."

Billy had always imagined Mighty Mamma to be well mighty. Not tiny and frail. The only pictures he had ever seen of her were the photographs on Dad's shop wall, all taken when she was very young and beautiful. Although she wasn't at all how Billy had imagined her, he knew straight away he liked her.

"Excuse me," said the steward, "but Billy's dad is supposed to be meeting him."

Mighty Mamma huffed. "So? He couldn't make it. I am here." And she handed the steward a letter.

"OK, everything's in order," said the steward, reading the letter. "Are you going to be all right, Billy?"

Billy nodded and said, "Fine."

"Santo!" shouted Mighty Mamma. "Over here!"

Billy looked up to see a mountain of a man coming towards them with a trolley and a beaming face.

"Mighty Mamma, he looks just like Pappa," said Santo. "Forgive us, Billy. Nice to meet you." He held out a huge friendly hand. "And welcome to the Big Apple."

"Where's Dad?" asked Billy when they were all packed into a taxi.

"He's tied up in a meeting," said Santo quickly, giving the taxi driver instructions. "Take the Williamsburg Bridge please, not the tunnel."

Somehow, Billy got the feeling that neither Mighty Mamma nor Uncle Santo was too pleased with Dad.

5

Santo's apartment was small and cosy with lots of pictures on the walls, just like Dad's barber's shop. Billy was looking at them when the doorbell rang. Uncle Santo went to answer it. A lady walked into the lounge. She had bright pink hair and looked just like a piece of candyfloss on a stick.

"Oh sugar!" squeaked the lady. "You must be Tony's boy! He looks like Tony's boy, don't you think?"

She walked up to Billy and pinched his cheek. Under her arm she was carrying a little dog wearing a pink jumper that matched her own.

"This is Miss Precious. She's a chihuahua. Don't you think she's a cutiepie?"

Miss Precious let out a piercing yap, showing a set of very sharp little teeth.

Mighty Mamma came out of the kitchen carrying a tray. "What are you doing here, Trixie?" she said sharply.

"It's just that Tony would like to see his son, and I thought I could kinda take him over to the apartment and, like, we could all get acquainted."

"Do you know my dad, then?" said Billy, surprised.

"You betcha, sweetiepie. Why, your dad and me are . . ."

"Coffee, Billy?" interrupted Mighty Mamma.

"No thanks, Mrs Piccoloni, it gives me tummy trouble," said Trixie.

"I wasn't asking you," said Mighty Mamma. "I think it's best you go. Santo will bring Billy along after he has had a little rest."

Whether it was the jetlag or whether it was because he was in a strange place, Billy wasn't sure, but he felt as if he was trying to put a jigsaw puzzle together with half the pieces missing.

As soon as Trixie had gone Billy asked Mighty Mamma, "Am I staying with you or with Dad?"

She took Billy's hands. "That's up to you," she said. "Why don't you see what you think when you've seen your dad?"

Dad's apartment was over a dry-cleaning shop and was nowhere near as nice or as cosy as Uncle Santo's. A familiar sound of yap-yapping could be heard coming from

another room. Dad looked
different somehow. He
was trimmer.

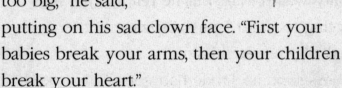

"Good to see your old
dad or what?" he said,
flinging his arms
round Billy and
trying to lift him off
the ground. "You're
too big," he said,
putting on his sad clown face. "First your
babies break your arms, then your children
break your heart."

Billy laughed. "I'm not a baby any more,
Dad."

"I know, I know. Well, what do you
think of New York? Isn't it just the ticket?"

Billy felt as if his dad was putting on a
show for his and Uncle Santo's benefit. He
hadn't asked Billy about Mum once.

A door opened and out came Trixie and
Miss Precious. The dog was yapping away,

this time dressed in a purple jumper with a bow on the top of her head.

"It's good to see you again, kid," said Trixie. "Hey, didn't I tell you, Tony? He's the spitting image of you!"

Dad looked a little sheepish. "Yeah," he said. "Why don't you go and fix Santo a beer, Trixie?"

"It can wait," said Trixie, putting her arms round Dad's neck and kissing him.

Billy felt angry. What was this candyfloss lollipop doing, hanging on to his dad like a brooch? Trixie looked at Billy and then at Tony. Dad seemed embarrassed.

"Well, are you going to tell him, honey, or shall I?" said Trixie, fluttering her long eyelashes.

"I think we should wait until Billy's settled in," said Dad, brushing her off. "He's only just arrived. Give the kid a chance."

"Tell me what?" said Billy angrily.

There was an awkward silence. Then Trixie squeaked, "I'm going to be your new stepmom."

6

Billy had not wanted to stay at Dad's after that. His stomach suddenly felt as if it were made out of lead. He knew his mum and dad weren't married but still, it didn't feel right his dad marrying someone else. Not so soon, anyway. And what about him and Mum?

Uncle Santo, seeing tears well up in Billy's eyes, rescued him by saying firmly, "I think the kid's tired. Perhaps this is not the right moment."

With that they left. Outside it was getting dark.

"Could we walk a bit?" asked Billy.

"Sure," said Santo. "Anyway, we'll have more luck getting a cab a couple of blocks up."

The street was busy and it had begun to rain when Billy saw a man standing in the

doorway of a shop. He was dressed in a long patched raincoat and perched on the top of his head he wore a toy witch's hat tied on with a piece of string. He smiled at Billy and said, "You want Double B batteries?"

Billy stopped and went over to look in the man's tray. It was full of batteries, all out of their wrappers. Each had written on them in spidery writing what they were, AAAAA batteries, CC batteries and so on. Billy couldn't see any Double B batteries anywhere.

"They're a dollar each," said the man.

"Have you really got Double B batteries?" said Billy.

"Yep," said the man. "Those are mighty special batteries. I don't put them on show for everybody, or else they would have all gone by now."

Billy had been given twenty one-dollar bills by Mum "just in case", and this was a just in case moment if ever there was one.

"No, Billy," said Uncle Santo, taking his hand and walking him away. "There are a lot of people in this city trying to sell you something. Just take no notice. Come on, I don't want you getting lost."

"Please," said Billy, pulling him back. "Dad gave me a money-box and it needs a Double B battery. I've got a dollar."

Uncle Santo was about to say there was
no such thing as a Double B battery, but
the look on Billy's face melted his heart.

"OK," he said, "but don't be too upset if it
doesn't work."

"You're in luck," said the man, handing
Billy the battery. "I've been keeping this
one back because it's so powerful. I hope it
brings you what you want."

On the battery were the words Double
B and in tiny faint writing "Not Long Life".

When they got back to Santo's apartment, Mighty Mamma had cooked a huge bowl of pasta.

"I'm sorry, Billy," said Mighty Mamma. "Santo, he tell me what happened. This is all very upsetting. It's very hard sometimes to understand why grown-ups make such silly mistakes."

Billy was feeling better and very sleepy now that he had eaten. It had been a long day. So much had happened, so much that he didn't understand.

Mighty Mamma tucked him up in bed.

"Oh," said Billy. "My battery. I didn't . . . " but before he could finish what he was saying, Billy Pickles was fast asleep.

7

In the morning Billy got out of bed,
unpacked his money-box carefully from his
rucksack, put in the battery and turned it
on. The smiling mouth opened and a tongue
shot out. It seemed a little disappointing if
that was all it did, especially after it had
taken him so long to find the right battery.
He read the instructions again and saw that
they said: "Place a dime on the tongue".

Mighty Mamma was sitting in front of
the TV when Billy asked her if he could
have a dime to put in his money-box.

"No good morning? Just dimes?" said
Mighty Mamma.

"Oh, I'm sorry. Good morning. It's just . . ."
and Billy told Mighty Mamma all about
Dad's present and how he and Santo had
found a man selling Double B batteries.

"Eh!" said Mighty Mamma, after hearing

Billy's tale, "I would like to see where my dime goes."

Billy brought the money-box into the lounge and placed it on the table near the TV. He put the dime on the tongue and it disappeared. They heard the coin clink. Then the money-box rubbed its tummy with one hand whilst holding the other out in front.

"I have never seen a money-box like that. What do you think it wants?" said Mighty Mamma. "Here, put another dime on its hand. Let's see if it does anything."

Billy did this and the hand threw the money into the money-box's mouth. Both Billy and Mamma were delighted.

"Well, who would have thought they could make a money-box do that! What will they think of next?" said Mighty Mamma.

They were both getting up to go into the kitchen to make some breakfast when the money-box spoke. It said, "562."

Billy went over to the money-box. "What did you say?"

The money-box said it again. "562."

"What does it mean?" said Mighty Mamma.

"I don't know," said Billy.

"Do you want another two dimes to see if it does it again?"

Billy took the dimes from his grandmother, but then he remembered what was written on the battery, "Not Long Life", so he turned the money-box off and put the dimes on the table. He would show it to his dad later.

Billy had breakfast and got dressed and forgot all about his talking money-box. Much more important was the fact that his dad was going to pick him up and show him New York. He couldn't wait. He would have a chance to talk to Dad properly and ask him all his "why" questions.

At one o'clock Dad still hadn't shown up. Billy sat on the sofa waiting with Mighty Mamma and watching the Katy Gee Guessing Game show.

"Now, my friends," said Katy Gee, "today we have the most yummy chocolate chip cake and your guess, viewers, is this. How many chocolate chips are in the cake? The prize for the lucky winner is a Magic Fix blender and there's a bonus prize if you get the number spot on. So what are you waiting for? The lines are now open."

"Where is Tony?" said Mighty Mamma. "He should have been here three hours ago."

"Why don't we phone up and say the money-box number?" said Billy.

Mighty Mamma looked at him. "Sorry about your dad, Billy. I will have strong words with him when he finally gets here."

"Mighty Mamma, please," said Billy. "Can we call the Katy Gee show and say 562 and see if the money-box is right?"

8

An hour later Billy and Mighty Mamma were being driven to the TV studios downtown to pick up their prize in person. The money-box had got the number spot on.

Katy Gee was delighted to see Billy and his grandma. "This is truly wonderful, Mrs Piccoloni. How did you guess the right number?"

"It was my grandson," said Mighty Mamma. She put an arm round Billy. "He has a way with the numbers." The audience clapped.

"And this is the first time you have been to New York?" said Katy Gee.

"Yes," said Billy.

The audience clapped again.

"What have you seen so far?"

"Your show and the view from a taxi,"

said Billy. "This is my first day."

"Billy Pickles," said Katy Gee, "we are about to change all that. The bonus prize is a ride for four people over Manhattan in a helicopter."

"Wow!" said Billy.

After the show was over they were taken on a tour of the studios. Then they had lunch with Katy Gee. She still could not get over how clever Billy and Mighty Mamma had been.

"You have no idea," she said, "how rare it is for anyone to get the number spot on. How did you do it?"

"It's our little secret," said Mighty Mamma, looking at Billy.

The day ended with a stretch limo driving them back to the apartment.

"Makes up a little for Dad not showing, eh?" said Mighty Mamma as they drove up Fifth Avenue.

"A little," said Billy, smiling.

9

Mighty Mamma and Billy put the Magic Fix blender on the kitchen table next to the yummy-looking chocolate cake from the studio.

"What's this, Mamma?" said Santo when he got home that afternoon.

"It is a present to you from Billy and me," said Mighty Mamma with a cheeky smile on her face.

"No, you shouldn't have, Mamma. There is no need," said Santo. "This machine is very expensive. You can't afford to go getting me presents, Mamma."

"I wish I could have bought it for you, Santo, but the truth is I didn't," said Mighty Mamma mysteriously.

"Then how come it's here if you didn't buy it?" said Santo.

"Go on, guess how many chocolate chips are in that cake," said Billy.

Santo scratched his head. "I don't know," he said, laughing.

"Go on," said Billy. "Guess."

"All right then, 283," said Santo.

"No," said Mighty Mamma, "there are 562 exactly!" Then she and Billy told him how they had won the blender and all about their extraordinary day. Santo was most impressed.

"How did you guess the right number?"

"It was the battery I bought," said Billy.

"No, it can't be," laughed Santo. "Anyway, Billy, who are you going to take on this helicopter ride?"

Billy said without a second thought, "I would like to take Mighty Mamma, and you and my friend Walter."

"What about your dad?" said Santo.

Billy shook his head. "Not Dad," he said. "He might not show up."

10

That evening Dad and Trixie turned up to take Billy out for a meal. Mighty Mamma was waiting for them in the hall. She took Dad by the ear, dragged him into the kitchen and shut the door. For the first time Billy caught a glimpse of why the word mighty went with Mamma. She sounded like a machine gun firing words off rat-a-tat-tat in Italian.

"It's a good thing we don't understand what they're saying," said Trixie, who was sitting on the sofa adjusting Miss Precious's leopardskin jacket and diamante collar. "Do you see, honey," she said to Billy, "how she matches my coat and my engagement ring? Don't we both look a picture?"

Billy said nothing. He wished he had
been taught Italian. After a few minutes
Dad came into the room, the smile wiped
off his face.

"Are you ready, Billy?" said Mighty
Mamma. "Your dad's taking you out to a
restaurant."

"Oh gee whizz, I sure could do with

something to eat," said Trixie, jumping up.

"No," said Mighty Mamma firmly. "Not you. I think Tony has some explaining to do to Billy first."

"I'm sure I could help," said Trixie, but one look at Mighty Mamma's face told her she would be eating alone.

Dad took Billy to a restaurant a few blocks away. They didn't speak much. Billy could see that Mighty Mamma's words were still whooshing around Dad's head, but he had recovered by the time they were seated and had ordered their food.

"This was the favourite haunt of Frank Sinatra," said Dad. "What do you think?"

Billy thought that the pastrami sandwich that turned up could have fed him and Mum for a couple of nights.

"Look, kid," said Dad, "I'm sorry. We got off to a bad start, but we're friends, right?"

Billy nodded. His mouth was too full to speak.

Dad looked uncomfortable.

"Billy, I wasn't cut out to be a small town barber in the middle of nowhere. You've got to understand. I have big ideas. Ideas need a city. This, buddy, is a big city, where fortunes are made on no more than a dream. I tell you, I have big dreams and I'm going to make them come true."

"Why did you leave Mum and me?" asked Billy.

Dad ignored what Billy had said and carried on. "I've got me a business partner, a great guy called Nathan Chance. He's Trixie's boss. He's from the big country, you know, where they wear cowboy hats and boots. He thinks my idea's a sure-fire winner and he wants to come in on it with me. Do you want to know what my idea is?"

Billy was looking down at the table. He didn't feel hungry any more. He just wished he was home with Mum.

"Wagon Trail tours!" continued Dad.

"Going along the same route as they did in the days of old but with all mod cons. What do you think?"

Billy sat there feeling unhappy. What had any of this to do with him or Mum?

"Come on, Billy. This is America. Aren't you excited? I'm going to be rich. We're all going to be rich."

"All I want to know," said Billy, fighting back the tears, "is why you left Mum and me and why you're going to marry Trixie."

Dad's ears had started to go red, just like Billy's did when he wasn't telling the truth.

"Your mum and me — how shall I put it? — grew apart. Hey, it happens. But look, kid, the most important thing is that we're here together in a restaurant that Frank Sinatra ate in. Doesn't that make you feel top of the heap? A number one?"

"No," said Billy. "It makes me feel sad."

"Come on! Cheer up. Tonight I'm in the money, so splash out and get yourself a

great dessert."

"No thank you," said Billy. "Can we go back to Santo's now?"

"Do you know how many wives Frank Sinatra had?" said Dad, getting the bill.

"What's that got to do with anything?" said Billy.

"Look, kid," said Dad. "There's a lot you don't understand. And I'm sorry but I want to tell you, to get the record straight." He put his hand out to touch Billy's shoulder. Billy moved quickly away.

"See, I love Trixie. She's a great girl and, well, she makes your old dad happy. Just try and be nice to her. She's got such a kind heart."

After that, Billy felt there was no point to his "why" questions. The whys just hung between them, angry and unanswered. Grown-ups, thought Billy, were a mystery.

They made their way back to Santo's apartment in silence.

Mighty Mamma opened the door and one look at Billy's face told her that things hadn't gone well. Billy went and sat in the lounge. He could hear Mighty Mamma saying, "So you will be here tomorrow, Tony, to take Billy out?"

"I can't," said Dad. "I've told you, I have to work. It's important, Mamma, that I get this right. Our future depends on it. I can't look after the kid as well. Come on, please help me out here."

Billy got up and went into his room. He didn't want to listen to any more. He sat on his bed, tears rolling down his face. He said aloud, "I wish I was home with Mum."

The money-box was on the side table and Billy turned it on and put a dime on the tongue. The money-box clanked it down, rubbed its tummy, and threw the other coin into its mouth. Even through his tears it made Billy smile. Then it said 26, 34, 12, 19, 21, 7 and, after another clink, 3. Billy wrote

the numbers down and turned off his money-box. He got undressed and into bed.

Mighty Mamma came in with some hot milk and a cookie. She sat on the bed next to Billy.

"Come here and let your old nonna give you a hug," said Mighty Mamma. "This hasn't been easy for you, has it?"

"No," said Billy.

"Sometimes grown-ups are a real disappointment," said Mighty Mamma. "They can be much more selfish and childish than children and that is bad because they are old enough to know better and they don't."

"The money-box came up with some more numbers," said Billy.

"It did?" said Mighty Mamma.

"Yes," said Billy. "I wrote them down." He showed them to Mighty Mamma.

She stared at them and said, "I told Tony to phone your mamma this evening and

51

tell her what's going on."

"Good," said Billy.

They sat on the bed together, looking at the money-box and listening to the hum of New York outside.

"I don't think the numbers can have anything to do with chocolate cake," said Billy after a while.

"I shouldn't think so," said Mighty Mamma. "It would be one giant cake to have so many chocolate chips in it, don't you think?"

Billy went to brush his teeth, then got into bed and snuggled up under the covers.

"I forget to tell you. I called Walter and he would love to come," said Mighty Mamma.

"Great," said Billy. "I wonder what those numbers mean?"

"I don't know, Billy," said Mighty Mamma. "Maybe it was luck that the money-box came up with the right numbers today. Maybe they don't mean anything. Maybe

they do. Who knows?"

She kissed Billy goodnight and turned off the light. In the darkness of the room, the money-box smiled at Billy. If only he knew how amazing those numbers would prove to be.

11

All Detective Jack Sherman from the New York City Police Department wanted was a quiet day and to get home in time for his daughter's sixth birthday. He certainly didn't want a constant headache over a safe. It had been pulled out of the Hudson River ten days earlier, and so far no one had managed to get it open.

It was not through lack of trying. The safe dated back to a bank robbery that had taken place in the 1920s. There were diamonds worth a small fortune inside. The newspapers had got hold of the story and it had captured the imagination of New Yorkers. Apparently the robbers had been defeated by the safe, and rather than be caught with it they had dumped it in the river. Now it sat in a room surrounded by guards and safe-breakers, none of whom

could get it open.

To make matters worse, the Chief of Police was breathing down Detective Sherman's neck.

"It's making the police department look stupid, not being able to open a safe from the 1920s," he growled.

Jack Sherman took a deep breath and started to explain for the hundredth time that this safe had been made by a master locksmith. He was famous for making the

safest safes in the world. There were apparently over a billion combinations. One of those would open the safe, but no one knew which. Detective Sherman had people working round the clock, but still they weren't anywhere nearer to solving the problem.

"I don't want a history lesson," yelled the Chief of Police. "Just get that safe open today. That's an order."

Oh heck, thought Detective Sherman. Weren't there more important things he could be doing than this? Like capturing the fraudster Spike the Spider, for example. This crook had been taking people's money under false pretences for years, but so far he had always managed to get away and pin the blame on someone else.

Jack Sherman was now on his third cup of coffee. He couldn't sit here all day, waiting for someone to break that darned code.

Suddenly he remembered what his wife

had said last night about an English kid with an Italian grandma who had guessed the right number of chocolate chips in a cake. "They got it spot on," she had said, "not just nearly right but one hundred per cent right. Don't you think that's remarkable?"

Detective Sherman picked up the phone. "Get me the Katy Gee show, please," he said.

12

The helicopter took off in a whirl, dipping out over the Hudson and towards the Statue of Liberty. They circled overhead looking down at the golden torch in her hand.

"Oh wow! That's something!" said Walter.

"Look," shouted Billy over the noise of the helicopter. "How small everybody is!"

"This is superb," said Mighty Mamma. "Santo, come look, you will never see your city like this again."

"Hey, Billy," said Santo, looking a little green. "All this for guessing the right number of chocolate chips!"

"Are you all right?" said Billy, seeing the worried look on Uncle Santo's face.

"I don't like heights," said Santo nervously.

They were now flying over Central Park. "I can see where I live," said Walter.

"That's the Dakota Building, home to the

rich and famous," said the pilot.

Billy looked impressed and said, "That must be nice." Walter didn't say anything.

"You wouldn't think Central Park was so big," said Mighty Mamma.

"The green lungs of New York, Mamma," said the pilot.

When they landed, Detective Jack Sherman was waiting at the heliport to greet them.

"Are you Mrs Piccoloni?" said Detective Sherman, holding out a hand towards her.

"What's Tony done now?" said Mighty Mamma.

"Sorry, lady, I don't know who Tony is. I am looking for you and Billy Pickles. I have a problem that you might be able to help me with."

"What's going on?" said Uncle Santo, who was still feeling a little wobbly on his legs. "We've done nothing wrong."

"I know," said the detective. "Look, this

may sound nuts to you, but let me explain."
He told them all about the robbery and the
safe. "It's a gamble," he said. "You might be
able to crack it or you might not. Frankly,
I'm so desperate I'd use smoke signals if I
thought they would work. Will you come
back to the precinct with me?"

Billy looked at Mighty Mamma.

"Excuse me," said Mighty Mamma, "I need to talk to my grandson alone."

They walked a little way off.

"Have you got those numbers?" said Mighty Mamma.

"Yes," said Billy, "but they might be wrong. They might be for something else."

"Billy," said Mighty Mamma. "Like I said last night, this whole thing might mean something or it might mean nothing. So, what have we got to lose?" She shrugged her shoulders just like Dad.

"OK," said Billy. "We could pick up the money-box on the way to the precinct. But what about Walter?"

"Don't worry," said Mighty Mamma. "Santo can take Walter back to the café and we can join them later."

When they arrived at the precinct, Billy and Mighty Mamma were taken to a room full of people and computers. On a table in

the middle sat the safe. A man was
listening to it with a stethoscope.

"It looks like they've all gone mad," Billy
whispered to Mighty Mamma. Detective
Sherman overheard him and laughed.

"Not far from the truth, kid," he said.
"Well, how do you want to work this?"

"How many numbers does it need?"
asked Billy.

"Five," said Detective Sherman.

"Single or double?"

"Single."

"I have to speak to Mighty Mamma alone," said Billy.

They walked over to a corner of the room. Everyone was looking at them.

"Then the numbers you got last night won't work," said Mighty Mamma.

"No," said Billy.

"We need to see if the money-box can give us the right numbers," said Mighty Mamma.

"We'd better put in another dime," said Billy.

"Scusi, we can't work with people watching us," said Mighty Mamma to everyone in the room, "so if you want us to help you, we need to be left alone. Could everyone leave the room, please, and let's see if we can get this thing open."

When everybody had left, Billy put the money-box on the top of the safe and fed

it the first dime. The money-box clinked it down and rubbed its tummy. It threw the other dime into its mouth. Then it said: "1 4 7 4 9."

Billy wrote the numbers down carefully on a piece of paper, turned the money-box off and was just putting it away in his rucksack when the door flew open and the Chief of Police came storming in, followed by Detective Sherman.

"Sherman, would you care to tell me

what these people are doing here? This is not a game show," said the Chief of Police.

"I know that, sir, but I thought they just might be able to help," said Detective Sherman.

"Would you like the number?" said Billy.

The Chief of Police snatched the piece of paper from Billy and walked up to the safe. He turned the dial, then pulled at the door. Nothing happened.

"Just as I thought. Sheer waste of time!" thundered the Chief of Police. "Sherman, you've got some explaining to do!"

At that moment there was a loud click and the dial on the front of the safe started spinning round and round. Then the huge door creaked open to reveal its gleaming treasure.

13

By the time Billy and Mighty Mamma had got back to Santo's café, they had already appeared on the early evening news. The boy who cracked the safe was the top story.

Santo got them all an ice cream while they sat watching the TV. The Chief of Police was saying that the breakthrough had been made possible by the superb work of Detective Sherman, who had the brains to think in an imaginative way and get hold of the kid who was good with numbers.

"Did you have a good time here?" said Billy to Walter.

"It's been great," said Walter excitedly. "Santo let me help serve in the café and we sold I don't know how many ice creams."

Mighty Mamma turned away from the TV and looked at Santo. "You didn't make the kid work for you," she said.

"Honestly, Mrs Piccoloni, it was the best day ever," said Walter.

"You know, this kid," said Santo, patting Walter on the back, "could sell ice creams to Iceland. He has the golden touch. I tell you, Mamma, I have never seen it in one so young. You can have a job any time, kid." They all laughed.

Just then the door opened and Trixie came tottering in on very high stiletto heels, accompanied by Miss Precious. Both were dressed in a mixture of greens and reds.

"Why, Billy, I've just seen you on TV!" cried Trixie. "Oh my, aren't you smart! How do you do it?"

"Are you going to sit down or stand there looking like a Christmas tree?" said Mighty Mamma.

Trixie sat down.

"This is Walter, my friend," said Billy. "Walter, this is Trixie. She works for my dad's business partner."

"My pleasure, I'm sure," said Trixie, brushing him aside. "I phoned Tony the minute I saw you and told him the whole story and he says he's coming over right away."

"I've got to go, Mrs Piccoloni. My driver's here," said Walter. "It's been a really great day, the best ever."

"It's been a pleasure, Walter, and you can call me Mighty Mamma," said Mighty Mamma.

"Any time," said Santo. "Any time, you can come and spend the afternoon with me."

"Could you come over to my place tomorrow, Billy? If that's all right with you, Mighty Mamma," said Walter.

"I'd love to," said Billy.

"That's all right with me," said Mighty Mamma.

"Thanks, Mighty Mamma. OK then, Billy, Arnold my driver will pick you up about ten," said Walter.

"That kid has a driver!" said Trixie, turning round to watch Walter leave the café. "You know, I'm sure I've seen him before in some magazine. What's his surname?"

"Minks," said Billy.

Trixie let out a shriek and nearly fell off her chair. "Oh my! I don't believe it! I have actually said hello to Marilyn Tinsel's boy!"

Both Mighty Mamma and Billy looked at Trixie as if she had lost her marbles.

"Are you all right?" said Mighty Mamma.

"Surely you've heard of Marilyn Tinsel? Why, everyone's heard of Marilyn Tinsel," said Trixie, all in a tizz.

"Apparently not," said Santo.

70

"She's in all the papers and magazines!" cried Trixie. "She was married to Walter Minks the Third."

"What are you talking about?" said Mighty Mamma. "Have a drink of water and calm down. Walter is just Billy's friend, that's all."

At that moment Billy's dad came in.

"Where's my boy? Where's the kid who cracked the safe? Two days in New York and you're already a star. What did I tell you, Billy?" He started singing his favourite Frank Sinatra song.

"Enough of Frank Sinatra," said Mighty Mamma.

Dad looked wounded and clutched at his heart. "You can never have enough of Ol' Blue Eyes," he said with feeling. He kissed Mighty Mamma on both cheeks.

"So, kid, tell your old dad the secret. How do you do it?"

"He doesn't," said Mighty Mamma.

Billy's heart gave a lurch. His grandma

wasn't about to give the game away, was she?

"We do it together," said Mighty Mamma. Now if you will excuse us, we are tired and we're going home."

"But I thought we could take Billy out for a meal," said Dad. "You know, paint the town red. What do you say?"

"I say no," said Mighty Mamma. "You were too busy to see your son yesterday. You were too busy to be with him today. Now he has been on TV, you suddenly have time. No," she repeated firmly. "Remember you have work to do. Don't let us keep you from it."

Billy felt pleased that Mighty Mamma had said no. Dad stood there looking hurt as she took Billy firmly by the hand and left.

Back at the apartment, Mighty Mamma made Billy a delicious supper. She laid the table with a checked tablecloth and lit the candles.

"This is like I do it back home when I
have guests," said Mighty Mamma.

"It's like a restaurant, only better," said
Billy.

Dessert was home-made chocolate
profiteroles. It was the best thing Billy had
ever tasted.

"Wow!" said Billy. "Thank you, Mighty Mamma."

Mighty Mamma smiled. "Your mum, she brought you up well, Billy. One day I would very much like to meet her."

"I wonder what those other numbers were for?" said Billy, licking the last bit from his spoon.

"I don't understand it," said Mighty Mamma, "but one thing I do know is that those numbers sure mean something. But what they mean — that is another question."

14

The apartment Walter lived in was like a film set. It had marble floors and oak-panelled rooms full of beautiful paintings.

There was even a grand staircase. A butler had let Billy in and a housekeeper had served them lunch.

Walter's room had pictures of pirates painted on the walls and a ceiling with a night sky on it that twinkled when you turned on the light. It was packed full of toys, just like a shop, and half of them were still in their boxes and wrappers. This, thought Billy, was something else, something unreal.

"You have the latest G5 Quantum game," said Billy. "Wow, it costs well — "

Billy stopped what he was saying and looked at Walter. He was sitting on his bed looking miserable.

"It was a bad idea you coming here. Now you'll think I'm a spoilt pig, like all the other kids do."

Billy went and sat next to him. "Don't be daft. I don't think that. I think you're grand."

"What does that mean?" said Walter.

"I think you're all right," said Billy. "It's just amazing to have so many toys and a room with paintings on the wall."

"I'd give them all away to have a family like yours, where you're wanted."

"Oh come on," said Billy. "Look at all this. Of course you're wanted, otherwise you'd have nothing, right?"

"Wrong," said Walter. "My dad's so busy that I have to make an appointment to see him. We always go out to a smart restaurant. He tells his assistant that he won't be taking any calls. We sit there and over lunch I tell him how well I'm doing at school and show him my report. If it's bad I don't get dessert. If his assistant interrupts us while we're having our quality time lunch together he goes ballistic." He pointed at all the unopened toys. "Go on, look at them. They all have stickers on them."

Billy looked and sure enough they all had girls' names written on them.

"Who are they all?" asked Billy.

"My dad's girlfriends. They all give me presents and the ones that are crossed out with a red marker are old girlfriends. You think your dad's bad, but mine is terrible. When we have one of our awful lunches I have to make sure I get the name of his current girlfriend right, otherwise he goes nuts."

"It sounds bad," said Billy. "What about your mum?"

"She's a movie star," said Walter. "She left me when I was five and moved to LA. She married a film director who can't stand children. He says they age stars terrible, so I am not allowed to be seen with Mum in public. I stay in a wing of their house away from everybody. They get me the latest games and DVDs, and there's a huge pool to swim in, but I would much rather they wanted to be with me."

"Well," said Billy, "Mum and me haven't

78

anything apart from — " Billy thought for a
minute — "I mean we're really poor."

"I'd love to have a family like yours,
where you're really wanted and you're not
just a parcel," said Walter.

"Would you like to know a secret?" said
Billy, who didn't like seeing Walter so sad.

"You promise you won't tell?"

"Promise," said Walter, cheering up.

Billy told him all about the money-box.

"That's amazing!" said Walter. "I'd love to see it working."

"I'm sure you can next time we meet," said Billy, "but the thing is, it says on the batteries 'Not Long Life', so I have to use it carefully."

15

Dad turned up alone the next day to take Billy out. He brought Mighty Mamma flowers and said he was sorry.

"Are we going up to the top of the Empire State Building?" asked Billy excitedly as they left the apartment.

"No," said Dad, "not today. My business partner, he's keen to meet you and I want to show you my office. What do you say?"

Billy felt it didn't matter what they did as long as it was just him and Dad. They got a cab downtown to his office. Billy's heart sank when they got out of the elevator and saw Trixie waiting for them. She was wearing a genuine cowgirl costume with rhinestones. Miss Precious had a matching outfit with a sheriff's badge.

"Welcome to The Past is Your Present Tours!" said Trixie.

Billy stared at her open-mouthed.

"Guess who I am. Go on," said Trixie.

"I haven't a clue," said Billy, looking
bewildered.

"It's so easy you'll kick yourself when I
tell you," said Trixie. "It's Annie Get Your
Gun, of course!"

Billy sighed. Mighty Mamma had told
him not to get his hopes up about today
and she couldn't have been more right.

Dad's office was the size of a broom cupboard. By the time all three of them were inside, it was hard to close the door.

"Small and compact, that's the way I like it," said Dad, sitting squashed behind his tiny desk.

"Where's your computer?" asked Billy.

"Don't need one," said Dad. "A mobile phone is all I need, and this." He took out a shoebox. In it was a model of an old-fashioned Wild West wagon.

This all seems to be getting sillier by the minute, thought Billy.

"I told you — we're selling wagon trail tours," said Dad. "So that you can travel like they did in days of old but with all the comforts that the twenty-first century has to offer. You can spend time eating round a campfire and sleeping under the moon and the stars."

"What about the bathroom?" said Trixie. "I mean, no one wants to do you know

what in the open."

"The finer details are being worked out as we speak," said Dad grandly. "But every day I get people buying one of our tours. What do you think, kid? Is it good or is it good?"

"When do they start?" said Billy.

"The first one is in a month's time. There's still a lot to do. Exciting, isn't it?" said Dad, beaming.

"But, honey, shouldn't you know what you are going to do about the bathroom by now?" said Trixie.

"Sweetie, don't worry your pretty little head," said Dad. "Tony Pickles has it all under control. There's a team of product designers in Chicago working on the wagons as we speak. Come on, Billy, let me introduce you to my business partner."

Nathan Chance's office was like the man, big. His snakeskin cowboy boots rested on the desk in front of him. His cowboy hat

was pushed back off his face. He wore
shades and was smoking a large cigar and
blowing out smoke rings.

"Howdy, kid," he said, slowly rocking

back and forth in his chair. "Your dad tells me you have a winning way with numbers. So OK, let's see how good you really are. What's nine times eight?"

"I don't know," said Billy.

"OK. Tony, what's the answer?"

"Sorry," said Dad, "it's just slipped right out of my head."

"Well, you're all hopeless and it proves my point. The boy's just had two lucky strikes, that's all," said Nathan.

"Seventy-two," said Trixie. They all turned to look at her.

"Well, I like the outfit, sugar," Nathan said. "OK, boy who's good with numbers, what's the number of the horse that will come in first in the 2.30 today?"

"Don't know," said Billy. He felt the way a fly caught in a spider's web must feel. This man gave him the creeps.

"It seems to me," said Nathan Chance, "that you're no different from every other

kid, sponging off his parents. That's why I don't have kids. People say kids are worth their weight in gold, but I've never met one like that."

Trixie let out a nervous laugh. "You don't mean that," she said.

"I sure do," said Nathan. "Kids and dogs," he said, staring hard at Miss Precious. "Both of them are a waste of space."

"Just you wait," said Trixie, who wanted Nathan to be impressed with Billy. "He's got friends in high places. Go on, honey, don't be shy. Tell Nat about Walter Minks Junior."

Billy jumped back as Nathan moved over towards him as fast and as silently as a spider. He looked hard at Billy.

"Are we talking about Walter Minks the Third's son Walter?" he said.

"Yes," said Trixie, pleased to see Nathan was paying attention.

"How do you know Walter?" said Nathan, taking off his shades to look more

closely at Billy. He had small eyes that seemed to look straight through you. Billy felt his insides go wobbly.

"Go on," said Dad, "tell Mr Chance how you came to meet Walter."

Billy was quiet.

"I'll tell you," said Trixie. "Billy met him on the plane. He lives in the Dakota Building. He has a driver and he is well loaded."

"Interesting," said Nathan, putting his shades back on. "Haven't you got work to do, Tony?" he went on. "Better let cowgirl here take Billy home."

"Sorry," said Dad when he and Billy came out of Nathan's office. "You'll have to run along with Trixie. I've a lot of work on at the moment, but I'll make it up to you later. You do understand, don't you?"

16

The day before her birthday party, Mighty
Mamma and Billy were having breakfast
together. The TV was on in the background.
Neither of them was paying much attention
to it. Then a picture of Walter flashed up on
the screen.

"The headlines this hour . . . " said the
presenter. "Walter Minks Junior has been
kidnapped. The ten-year-old son of Marilyn
Tinsel and the multi-millionaire newspaper
tycoon Walter Minks the Third was
kidnapped last night outside the Dakota

Building where he was staying with his father."

Billy and Mighty Mamma stopped eating and stared at the TV.

"Walter Minks the Third," the presenter went on, "personally handed over the sum of three million dollars in the early hours of this morning and was assured that his son would be released at eight o'clock. So far there has been no sign of the child, and there has been no further communication from the kidnappers."

"This is terrible," said Mighty Mamma. "It gives me shivers in my bones to think that there are such nasty people in the world. Who would dream of doing that to a child?"

"This is really gross," said Billy. "Walter will be so frightened. What's going to happen to him?"

The doorbell rang and Billy went to open it. Trixie walked in, looking ghastly.

"I haven't slept a wink," she said. "I'm

afraid that Tony is in big trouble and the
worst thing is, he don't know it."

"Sit down, Trixie," said Mighty Mamma.
"You are making no sense."

There was a loud yelp as Trixie sat down
on Miss Precious. "Oh sorry, honey," she said,
lifting the dog up and giving it a kiss.

"This must be serious," said Billy to
Mighty Mamma. "Look, Miss Precious isn't
wearing any clothes."

"OK, Trixie," said Mighty Mamma, "why
don't you tell us nice and slowly what's
going on."

"Yesterday," said Trixie, "Nathan sent my Tony to Chicago to see the factory where the wagons are being made."

"So what's wrong with that?" said Mighty Mamma.

"Well, Tony calls me to say he's in Chicago and he just can't find the joint. I phoned Nathan to see if Tony has the right address. Well, I call and call. No answer, so I go round to the office. Now this is the strange part. There is no more office. It's all closed up. I can't get in because the locks have been changed and no one in the building knows anything."

Miss Precious started yelping.

"Oh, quiet, baby," said Trixie. "I tell you, that got me thinking. It's hard for me to say this, but I think that there are no wagons being made. I think Nathan has had Tony selling vacations that don't exist."

"If you are right, Tony is in big trouble," said Mighty Mamma.

"We could go to the police," said Billy.

"I will phone that nice detective Billy and I met," said Mighty Mamma. "He'll be able to help us."

"No," said Trixie, standing up, "you mustn't do that, Mrs Piccoloni."

"Why not?"

"Because I think everything has just got a whole lot worse. I think my boss, Nathan Chance, has kidnapped Walter."

"That's ridiculous," said Mighty Mamma. "What has your boss got to do with it?"

"It's just a feeling me and Miss Precious have in our bones. It's like the puzzles I do. It's all fitting together," said Trixie. "Alarm bells started to ring when I spilled the beans about Walter and the Dakota Building and everything. I just wanted him to be impressed with Tony's boy. I was so stupid to say that Billy knows Walter because if you think about it he's the perfect kid to kidnap."

"I bet it was him," said Billy. "He was like a spider. He gave me the creeps."

"I've always known that Nathan is one to take a chance," Trixie went on. "It's easy for him to clean up with all the money and lay the blame on Tony. Tony ain't smart with figures, you know."

Mighty Mamma and Billy sat down. Neither of them said a word.

"I can't get hold of Tony," said Trixie. "And I am sure worried about Walter. I mean, Nathan Chance doesn't like kids or dogs. He said so, didn't he?"

Billy nodded and Miss Precious yapped loudly. "You agree with me that we got to do something?"

"I still think we should call Detective Sherman," said Mighty Mamma.

"Wait," said Billy. "I have an idea."

17

Billy put the money-box on top of the TV and turned it on. The presenter was saying, "There is still no news on the whereabouts of Walter Minks, the child kidnapped yesterday. For the latest on the story we are going over live to LA and to Walter Minks's mother, Marilyn Tinsel." The camera focused on a very beautiful weeping woman. Her husband stood next to her.

"How do you feel?" said the reporter.

"My wife is too upset to speak," said the man. "That kid meant the world to us. We are flying to New York immediately. The police think he is still being held somewhere in the city, even though the ransom money has been paid."

"I just want my boy back. I'd give up all my fame to have him back," said Marilyn Tinsel tearfully. She was led away by her husband.

"That poor boy," said Mighty Mamma. "Where can he be? Finding him in this town is going to be like looking for a needle in a haystack."

"Do you think my money-box can help?" said Billy.

"Let's try it, Billy." And Mighty Mamma handed Billy two dimes.

Billy looked at Trixie. "You promise you won't tell a soul about this."

"I don't know what I'm promising but

OK, I promise," said Trixie.

The money-box stuck out its tongue. The first dime went clink and the money-box rubbed its chubby tummy.

"Oh, isn't that so cute!" said Trixie.

"Shhh," said Billy and Mighty Mamma together.

Now the money-box held out its hand for the second dime, threw it into its mouth and said, "Seven." Billy wrote the number down. Then it said, slightly slurring its words, "23." There was another longer pause after which it said slowly "14," followed by "3" and then "302." They all waited but the money-box had no more numbers to give. Billy quickly turned it off.

"I think it's running out of power," he said sadly.

"I get it," said Trixie, "the money-box gave you the numbers for the cake and the safe."

"Yes," said Billy, "but it also gave us some numbers that didn't mean anything."

"Give me the numbers you just wrote down, kid," said Trixie. And to Mighty Mamma's and Billy's complete surprise, she suddenly gave a whoop!

"I know! The kid's hidden somewhere in New York, right, but where? How do we find the location? Your money-box numbers give us the lead. Look." She produced a map of New York. "First of all, seven. We'll go to Seventh Avenue. Now," she said, following the route with her finger, "we'll cross at 23rd Street and look for number 14. If it's a hotel, 3 will mean the third floor and the last three numbers could mean the room. OK, Room 302!"

"What are we waiting for?" shouted Mighty Mamma, grabbing her coat and handbag. "Come on, and don't forget to bring the money-box with you, Billy."

They flagged down a yellow cab which screeched through the streets of New York and pulled up outside a run-down hotel.

A coachload of Italian tourists were checking in. Suitcases and arguments were cluttering up the lobby so that it was easy for them to slip unnoticed into an elevator and press the button for the third floor.

A long straight corridor with doors on either side led off the lobby. A linen trolley was parked halfway up it but there was no one in sight. Room 302 was near a flight of stairs.

"What now?" said Billy.

Mighty Mamma walked back to the trolley and took some clean towels off it.

"You stay here with Billy out of sight,"

she said to Trixie. "I'll go and see who's in there. Then if the money-box has got it right, we call Detective Sherman."

Mighty Mamma knocked on the door of Room 302. "Housekeeper!" she announced. Nothing happened. She knocked again. Finally a tough-looking man opened the door.

"What do you want?" said the man rudely. "Can't you read the sign? Do not disturb."

"Scusi," said Mighty Mamma, "but I have a job to do and someone asked for clean towels."

"Boss, did you order clean towels?" called the man.

"No, Sharky, I did not," came a voice that both Billy and Trixie recognised at once. So did little Miss Precious, who leapt out of Trixie's arms and ran yapping past Mighty Mamma, straight at the legs of Nathan Chance. What happened next happened so fast that neither Mighty Mamma nor Trixie had time to work out what they were doing. They just acted.

Taking aim, Mighty Mamma brought her handbag down hard on the head of Sharky, who went down like a boxer in the ring, out cold.

Miss Precious still had her teeth firmly in Nathan Chance's leg. Trixie rushed to help.

"Take that, you creep!" she shouted, giving Nathan a good biff. He reeled and was about to bash her back when Mighty Mamma gave him a knockout blow with her handbag. Nathan tottered, wobbling from side to side, and then crashed down on top of Sharky.

Billy pushed past them both and found Walter tied up in the bedroom.

"Wow, am I glad to see you! How did you know I was here?" said Walter.

"It's a long story," said Billy, untying him. "Are you all right?"

"Yes," said a very relieved Walter. "I thought I wasn't going to get out alive. That man was a really nasty piece of work."

"I know," said Billy.

"Tell me how you found me," said Walter.

"It was the money-box," said Billy.

"No," said Walter. "Really? That's amazing."

18

Detective Jack Sherman couldn't have been more surprised by the sight that greeted him as he entered Room 302. There were little Mrs Piccoloni and a lady he had never seen before, sitting on top of two large men while a small dog ran yapping round them. On the bed sat Walter and Billy drinking cola. They were all talking away as if it were a party.

"Hey!" said Detective Sherman, who was more than delighted to see that Walter was safe. "Sorry to interrupt you, but would someone care to tell me what's going on?"

It was Mighty Mamma who told the detective the story, while Trixie filled in the titbits.

"That's bad," said Walter when he heard that Billy's dad worked for Nathan Chance.

"The thing is," said Trixie, "Tony didn't know what Nathan was up to. He thought Nathan was interested in his Wild West Wagon Trail Tours, nothing else. And I didn't know what was going on either. Although I used to type his letters and answer the phone, he would never let me look at the files."

Detective Sherman listened attentively. Then he asked Walter, "Are you OK?"

"Yes, I'm just so pleased Billy found me."

"So am I," said Detective Sherman, leaning down to get a closer look at the

two men lying on the floor. "You're under arrest," he said, clapping on the handcuffs and pulling them to their feet. When he saw Nathan Chance's face, he smiled. "Well, well," he said. "What have we got here? If it isn't Spike the Spider!"

"Spike the Spider!" shrieked Trixie. "Do you mean I've been working for Spike the Spider?"

"Call my lawyer," said Nathan. "You won't be able to prove a thing."

"He can't be Spike the Spider, Detective Sherman," said Billy. "He's Nathan Chance, Trixie's boss. He's the man who . . . "

"Billy," said Detective Sherman, "this is none other than the fraudster Spike the Spider, alias Nathan Chance, and I've been after him for a long time. I've never been able to pin anything on him because he always manages to do a runner, leaving someone else to take the blame."

"You ain't got no proof," snarled Spike

the Spider, standing unsteadily on his feet. "If you want to know where your money is, you'd better ask Tony Piccoloni. I can tell you," he said, looking at Billy, "your dad is well and truly trapped in my web."

"Tony ain't got no three million dollars!" shrieked Trixie. "You think I'd be working for this creep if he had three million dollars?"

"Calm down, lady," said Detective Sherman. "I think we all need to go down to the precinct."

"Tony," said Mighty Mamma, "he is what you might describe as more of a child than Billy here. He may be stupid but he wouldn't knowingly be involved in anything criminal."

"That's right," said Trixie. "I can vouch for that."

"Mrs Piccoloni," said Detective Sherman kindly, "I am sure what you are saying is the truth, but it doesn't look good."

"Please," said Billy. "If we could find the

money, would that help?"

Detective Sherman sighed. "It would be a start."

"The money-box!" shouted Walter excitedly. Then he said, "Oh sorry, Billy. I shouldn't have said that."

"What?" said Detective Sherman.

"I found Walter because of my money-box," said Billy. "It gave me the numbers and Trixie worked out what they meant. That's how we're here. Maybe it could find out where the money is hidden."

Detective Sherman looked at Billy. "OK, I owe you one for getting that safe open. Go on, kid, get the money-box and let's see what it comes up with."

Billy placed the money-box on the table. He put one dime on the tongue. It moved slowly and there was a dull clink as it swallowed the dime. Then, even more slowly, it rubbed its tummy and held out its hand.

The second coin just made it into the mouth. Then there was a silence that seemed to go on forever.

Just when they all thought the money-box would never say anything ever again, it began to speak. Very, very slowly it said, "Forty-five." Then it said, "45 6 245," and then the money-box's smiling mouth shut tight.

"Do it again," said Detective Sherman, disappointed. "I don't think those numbers mean anything."

Billy tried again, but the money-box's smiling mouth was firmly shut. "I think it's run out of batteries," said Billy.

"I think we'd all better get down to the precinct and get Walter reunited with his parents," said the detective.

"Wait please," said Walter. "What's important on 45th Street?"

"It's a long street, honey," said Trixie, looking disappointed.

"If my memory serves me right," said

Detective Sherman, "on the corner of 45th Street and 6th Avenue there's Mini Apple Storage."

"That's it!" cried Trixie. "Me and Miss Precious are sure that's it!"

"That's what?" said Billy.

"The last number could be a storage unit, honey," said Trixie.

"Come on, everyone, what are we waiting for?" said Detective Sherman.

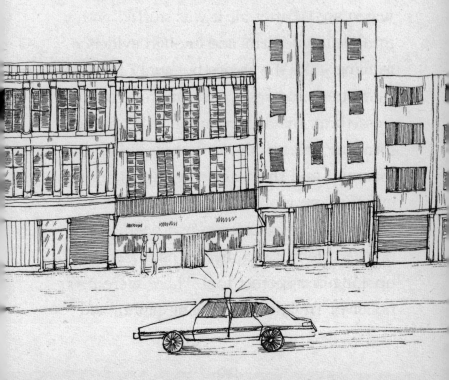

19

When they first arrived at Mini Apple
Storage it hadn't looked all that promising.
One sad old sofa was all there was in
lockup 245, and nothing else. According to
the guy on the desk it had just been
delivered that morning.

In the end it turned out that that old sofa
wasn't so sad after all. It was stuffed with
three million dollars and enough evidence
to have Spike the Spider put away for good.

Walter's parents were genuinely thrilled
to see him. His dad said that all his money
meant nothing without Walter, and even
his mum said she was going to make a real
effort to see more of him.

Tony's trip to Chicago had been a
disaster. He realised that he had been set
up. He felt a perfect fool. There were no
holidays. He had been selling hot air. A

very unhappy Tony Pickles made his way to the precinct to give himself up. The Chicago police questioned him for hours before they let him go, but the information he gave them was what they needed. They told Tony he was the wrong man in the wrong place at the wrong time.

"I'm sorry," he said to Billy when they were reunited, "I've made a mess of everything. But I promise you, kid, I'm going to turn over a new leaf."

"I don't understand why you left Mum and me to come here in the first place," said Billy.

"I don't understand it myself. I'd got myself into so much trouble with the money I owed, I suppose I thought it would be easier to start again. I had dreams of making it big like Frank Sinatra and then giving your mum back the money I lost."

"Why did you give me a money-box?" asked Billy.

"I sent away for it from a catalogue. I wanted you to be better with money than I am. I know you think I should have stayed with your mum, but I couldn't. I'm so sorry," said Dad. "I wanted to live life my way and it all went wrong."

"What about Trixie?" said Billy.

"You don't like her, do you?" said Dad.

Billy put his arms round him.

"Guess what," said Billy, "I like Trixie very much. I even quite like Miss Precious."

"You're a good boy, Billy. What did I do to deserve such a great boy as you?"

Billy shrugged his shoulders and put on a clown face, and Dad started to laugh.

Mighty Mamma's seventieth birthday party was a huge success. Detective

Sherman came with his family. Katy Gee showed up. Walter was there with his dad, though his mother had to fly back for a film she was making.

"But you know what," said Walter to Billy, "at least they're speaking. I mean, before they couldn't even be in a room together unless their lawyers were present." Billy laughed.

Santo had made an ice-cream cake shaped like the Statue of Liberty and afterwards there was dancing.

"Mrs Piccoloni," said Detective Sherman as he whirled Mighty Mamma across the floor, "there is one thing I would like to ask you. How did such a delicate lady as yourself manage to knock out two hardened criminals with a handbag?"

Mighty Mamma laughed out loud. "I always keep a paperweight in it. You never know who you might bump into."

At midnight they all sang Happy Birthday and raised their glasses to Mighty Mamma.

She climbed up onto the platform with the orchestra and, surrounded by her family, thanked all the guests for coming.

"This has been a wonderful trip," said Mighty Mamma. "I met my grandson Billy for the first time and I love this city. There is only one thing more to say. Tony, over to you."

She looked at Billy's dad who grabbed the microphone and belted out his favourite Frank Sinatra song: "New York! New York!"

20

The thing about adventure is that it is very hard to get back to normal when it's all over. Billy was thrilled to see Mum again and to tell her about what had happened to him and his famous money-box, but after a week the excitement of being back wore off.

Home seemed rather grey and drab after New York. Everything was just the same as it had always been: nothing had changed. Mum still worked too hard and her lady customers still complained about having their hair done in a barber's chair.

It was, thought Billy, as though he had never been away. The money-box sat on the window-sill again with two dimes beside it, a reminder of his last day with Dad when they had gone off together in search of the battery seller.

Much to their delight they had found him. But when Billy asked for Double B batteries the man smiled and said, "Kid, I never had no Double B batteries. Long life or short life, there ain't no such thing."

Dad wrote to Billy every week now. In his last letter, he had said that he had a steady job working with Santo in the café and that Trixie sent her love.

Billy and Walter talked a lot on the phone. Walter was very keen for Billy to come out next summer to spend time with him and his dad. "Things really are better," said Walter. "When I went to stay with my mum she took four days off filming just to spend time with me. It was great."

"It's hard," said Mum one Saturday afternoon after Billy had got off the phone and was looking down in the dumps. "You miss Dad and Trixie and Mighty Mamma and Santo, don't you?"

"No," said Billy untruthfully.

"Don't be daft, Billy. Of course you do. It's only normal."

"I love being here with you. It's just that I wish that they weren't so far away. It costs so much money to see them," said Billy sadly.

"I know, love. I wish there was something we could do about it but we just can't afford the fares."

"Do you mind about Trixie?" said Billy.

He hadn't asked his mum that question before.

"No," said Mum. "The best thing that happened between your dad and me was you. I'm happier on my own. He can't help being as daft as a Bakewell tart." They both laughed.

The radio was on in the background. "It's a rollover on the Lotto this week," said the announcer.

"You know, Mum," said Billy. "I've been thinking about those numbers the money-box gave me in New York. You know, the numbers that didn't mean anything."

"What about them?" said Mum.

"Well, I think we should give them a try. Maybe they were meant for when I got home."

"Can you remember what they were?" said Mum.

"There were seven of them," said Billy. "And I wrote them down. Let me find my

notebook. Look — 26, 34, 12, 19, 21, 7, 3."

"Well then, Billy Pickles," said Mum, "I think, with seven numbers and it being a Saturday, that we should buy a lottery ticket."

That evening, they were sitting in front of the TV with their fish and chips on their laps waiting for the lottery numbers to come up.

"Ladies and gentlemen, it's a rollover," said the TV presenter, "and here comes the first ball — number 26!"

Billy felt the hairs on the back of his neck stand up and he knew, as he watched first one then another ball come rolling down, that their lives were about to change.

"Number 34! Number 12! Number 19! Number 21! Number 7! And here comes the Bonus Ball," shouted the presenter.

Billy watched as the final ball, Number 3, slid into view.

Mum leapt up and shouted for joy. She and Billy danced round the room.

"We've won!" she cried. "The money-box has come up trumps. I can have a proper hairdressing salon. We can buy a house of our own. We can go on holiday to Italy and visit Mighty Mamma. Oh Billy," said Mum, tears of joy running down her cheeks, "what do you say?"

"I say," said Billy, with the biggest grin ever on his face, "I say our number has come up, and this time, Mum, it really is the right one."

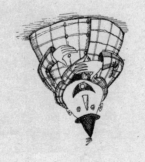

It's time to flip
the book for
another
magical story!

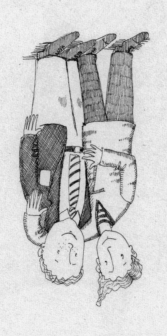

It's time to flip
the book for
another
magical story!